D.E. McCluskey

THE SPECIAL STUFF

THE SPECIAL STUFF
©2022 by D.E. McCluskey

ISBN# 9798351736037

First Edition

Cover, layout and interior
K. Trap Jones

www.theevilcookie.com

**For the
Mothers of Mayhem...**

Chicken kebabs or donna—it doesn't matter.
You girls are the spiciest meat between the folds
of my pita I could ever imagine!

CHAPTER
—1—

"So, I told him where he could stick his fucking parking ticket, and the fucking nonce, right, he told me he was recording this altercation for *his* safety!"

"What an arsehole," Finn replied, shaking his head. "Give a cunt a uniform and they all think they're Hitler."

"Tell me about it. So, I was about to grab him. I was gonna give him a proper kicking—"

"It's nothing more than shite like him deserve, mate," Finn interrupted his friend's diatribe.

"But," Mick continued, ignoring the interruption, and pointing at his friend, spilling a bit of his beer down the front of his shirt, "I thought better of it because those cameras, the ones on their chests, connect to the cloud, don't they? Everything they film, It's up there," he continued, pointing his half empty glass towards the dirty brown ceiling of the pub. Finn's eyes followed the glass as he took another long swig from his own pint, spilling most of it down his shirt. "Everything. He's got my eye, rectal fucking recognition thingy going on. He's got my profile, probably my bastard DNA too. So," he continued, pushing his glass into his friend's chest, spilling more of it and adding to the already spreading damp patch on Finn's beige sweater, "I decided against kicking the prick's head in, and I took the fucking ticket like a good, honest citizen!"

"Probably best," Finn replied, nodding while attempting to swig his drink again. "Bastards only have to give a little whistle and you'd have had a load of the wankers down on you, giving you a kicking, and you can bet that their fucking cameras wouldn't be working then, eh?"

Mick downed the last of his drink, burped, and pointed at his friend again, swaying on his heels. "Exactly. It's one rule for them and another for the rest of us," he slurred.

"You having another?" Finn asked, routing through his pockets, confident there was money in there somewhere. He'd been paid today, and knew he'd brought enough with him for a decent session with his oldest, best mate. It just seemed to be lost somewhere in the expanses of his many pockets.

"Yeah, just one more, though. I told Paula I'd be home handy."

"What time's handy?" Finn asked, finding the elusive twenty-pound note he knew had been hiding in there somewhere.

"Eightish."

Finn looked at his watch and laughed. "Well, you're pretty much fucked then, mate. It's almost ten!"

Mick reached for the jacket that was hanging on the back of his chair. He almost missed. He reached for the inside pocket and fished out his mobile phone and looked at the screen. "Shit!" he spat, a little louder than he wanted. The screen informed him there were seven missed calls from PAULA–WIFE. He closed his eyes and cursed under his breath. He put the phone back in his pocket and smiled at his mate. "One more then, eh?" he slurred.

Finn was ahead of him and already up from his seat. He staggered and fell back a little, banging into the table next to him, where an older couple were nursing their drinks, minding their own business. As he knocked the table, he knocked over the man's glass. Almost a full pint of dark ale soaked the table, spilling like a dark tsunami over the unassuming couple. The man jumped up and wiped himself down as his wife, her pink coat ruined by the liquid, cursed.

"Watch it," the old man muttered as Finn corrected himself.

His head whipped towards him. "What?" he hissed, his eyes blazing, his voice filled with venom and bile.

"I said watch what you're doing. Look at that," the older man replied, pointing towards his wife, who was now standing, holding out her coat to drip.

"I didn't do that, you senile old cunt," he hissed back. "You fucking did it yourself with your shitty shaking hands." Finn shook his own hands in an exaggerated manner, mocking him.

The man glared as he helped his wife with her coat. He shook his head at the younger man.

A fire roared in Finn's belly, and he knew he needed to vent it before it consumed him. "Don't you fucking shake your head at me, you old bastard. I don't care if you fought a fucking war for me."

"Now come on," the man replied, holding his hand out towards Finn. "There's no need for language like that, there's ladies present."

Finn looked at the old woman and laughed. "Ladies?" he asked. "Where? All I can see is this old mutt!"

"Eh, come on, that's enough," the old man warned, standing up straight and looking at him, straight in the eye.

"Enough?" Finn asked, forgetting all about going to the bar. Adrenaline was surging through his body, mixing with the alcohol, and the prospect of a fight, even with an old man, was spurring him on. He puffed out his chest and took a step closer to the old man, who was at the very least twice his age.

"Enough," Mick interrupted.

Finn watched the man's wide eyes shift from him towards Mick, his potential saviour.

Mick reached out a hand and pushed the old man's chest, knocking him down into his seat. He pointed at the old couple, his lips pulled right back, making his face a rictus of hate and anger. "Why don't you just shut the fuck up, drink what's left of your drink, take your old whore here, and fuck the fuck off?" he whispered, leaning in so his nose was almost touching the older man's.

Something about Mick's proximity must have spoken to him. He picked up his coat and took his wife's arm. "Come on, love, we're leaving."

Mick stood up and flashed an ugly smile towards them as they hurried off. She was struggling to get her arms into her ruined coat as her husband dragged her towards the exit. "That's the Dunkirk spirit," Mick shouted after them before sitting back down at his own table and draining the rest of his drink.

Finn was still laughing as he got to the bar.

"I'm not serving you, mate," the large bald man behind the counter stated, folding his arms and staring at him.

"What?"

"You heard me. I just watched you with that old fella over there. I'm not serving you."

"This is a bit fucked up," Finn slurred, looking all around, hoping to rally some of the other patrons of the bar to his cause. All he got in return was the backs of people's heads as they turned away, wanting no part of what was happening. "We only want one more, then we're off," Finn continued, grabbing hold of the bronzed bar around the underneath of the counter to stop himself from staggering backwards.

The barman leaned forward and looked him in his eyes. "I said, I'm not serving you, or your dickhead mate over there. Now, kindly fuck off, and don't let that door bang you on the arse as you go!"

Finn looked back to Mick, hoping to attract his attention and get the backup he so desperately needed. However, Mick was too busy on his mobile phone to notice him. "Mick," he shouted. "This bell-end won't serve me, mate."

"What?" Mick shouted back, squinting up from his phone.

"This dickhead won't serve me."

"You're drunk," the barman added.

"We're in a fucking pub," Mick replied. "What do you expect us to be?"

Finn shrugged and hitched his thumb over his shoulder towards the big man behind the bar. Mick blinked, adjusted his head, and looked where his friend was indicating. The huge, muscular barman had his arms folded and was scowling.

"Ah, fuck it off then," he slurred. "It's shit in here anyway!" He shouted this just loud enough for the barman to hear. The big man shifted his head, just a touch, but it was enough to indicate that Mick and Finn were no longer welcome in the Rose and Crown. "Come on, Finn. I'm starving anyway."

Finn made his way from the bar, towards their table. He felt a little like a tennis player who had just lost his big match in Wimbledon and was having to walk through the crowd to get out. Every pair of eyes in the bar were on him.

"Yeah, well... fuck you," Mick shouted as he made it to the exit.

A pang of terror tore through Finn as he pulled the door to get out and it wouldn't open. He looked back at Mick, who was jeering at the man behind the bar, offering him suggestive hand gestures and telling him what he thought of the big man's mother.

"It's locked," Finn whispered.

Mick shoved him aside and pushed the door. As it opened out into the cold night and the rain-soaked breeze hit his face, Finn relaxed. He turned back towards the barman and stuck two fingers up to him.

"Bell-end," he shouted as they both fell out onto the street.

The night air hit Finn like a slap to the face. Suddenly, the many pints of beer they'd sank that evening effected his legs, and he could feel them bucking beneath him. "Christ, Mick. It's freezing out here," he chattered.

"It's all right," Mick replied, digging his hands deep into his pockets and lowering his head against the biting wind. "Come on, I'm starving."

Up ahead in the gloom of the night, there was a small oasis of lights, one of them comprised of a large, red illuminated sign. The writing was yellow. It was the universal sign for a kebab shop.

***

It was called Ozzies. The sign outside proclaimed that it specialised in *the finest Turkish Cuisine*. It emphasised this by displaying many pictures of delicious and exotic looking dishes, mostly of mixed meat, lamb, and chicken. However, not one of these delicious, colourful meals were represented on the grimy, ill-illuminated menu that ran the length of the shop above the counter.

Finn shivered as they entered the greasy but welcoming warmth. The smell of cooking meat mixing with the fat dripping from the huge leg in the corner of the window set Finn's stomach singing. It was gurgling and bubbling in response to the delectable stench of weeks-old cooking oil. He knew he was hungry; he just didn't know he was this hungry.

"Fucking old bastard!" Mick was still griping, a full five minutes after being expelled from the pub. "I'm telling you, if that prick had been twenty years younger, I'd have kicked his fucking head in."

Finn wasn't listening; his mouth was watering, and his stomach was shouting at him, ordering him to fill it, as he eyed the revolving slab of meat, surrounded by a vertical gas cooker. It was spinning slowly, cooking the outside layer of the thick, dripping cylindrical leg.

"Oi, you, fuckface," Mick shouted at the small man in the back of the shop, who had his back to them.

The man ignored Mick's greeting.

"Hey, I shouted you, you fucking greasy prick," he called again.

This made Finn laugh. Mick always had a way with words, especially after a few beers.

The small, bearded man looked up from wiping down the ovens in the back. He gave a smile at his two customers. There was no love in that smile at all. It looked like the man's mouth wanted to greet these men, but all the niceties of the night failed to reach his eyes.

"Good evening, gentlemen," he said, broken English obvious as he flashed crooked, yellowing teeth between his hairy lips.

"Cut the patter and give us two doner kebabs and chips," Mick snapped but mostly slurred.

"And don't skimp on the chilli sauce," Finn added, mimicking Mick's lead. "We don't want any of your horrible shite either, just the good stuff," he continued.

Mick's face broke into a drunken leer. "And wash your hands before you do it, you filthy cunt. I know what your kind do with your hands... scratching your balls and your arse, and that."

The small man just stared at the drunken louts, his eyes flicking slowly between them.

"Chop chop..." Mick said, shooing him with his hands.

Finn laughed. "Cover them with mayo too, so we don't have to taste how bad they are," he ordered.

"Hey, Ozzie?" Mick asked, pointing at the slab of kebab meat, spinning and dripping. "What is that elephant leg made out of anyway? Your missus?" he continued, cracking up at his own joke. "Or is it the kids?"

"I wouldn't fucking touch this shite if I wasn't this pissed. I bet It's made from cocks and arseholes," Finn added, cracking Mick up even more. He looked at his friend, grinning, happy that Mick was almost creased over laughing, so he carried on. "Yeah, give me one of those arsehole kebabs, you filthy camel jockey."

The small man looked at the two drunken customers. His face was stoic, devoid of any emotion. The only thing that differentiated him from a mannequin in a department store was that his head was nodding, just slightly.

"They're special lamb," he explained eventually. "The meats are infused with a number of herbs and spices." Then a smile broke on his face, not just a small smile but a huge grin, one that almost spread from ear to ear. "But, my friends, what I am giving you tonight is the *special stuff*. It's a meat called Metagh. I only reserve it for my special customers. Please, I hope you enjoy it, my friends."

At the mention of the word Metagh, a head popped around the partition from the back of the shop. The man looked a lot like Ozzie, but where Ozzie's hair and beard were black with greying flecks, this man's were pure silver, contrasting with the olive hue of his skin. He looked at Ozzie before casting his eyes over the two drunken men.

He squinted as he spoke. It was fast, and it was foreign. Ozzie replied, talking equally as fast, nodding, and gesturing with his hands, pointing at the swaying men before waving his hands in the air theatrically.

The newcomer shook his head. He then let out a slow sigh, shrugged, and looked the two customers over again. He frowned before disappearing back into the kitchen, still shaking his head.

"I don't care what you call it," Mick slurred, undeterred by the rapid-fire conversation. "Just give me it and we'll fuck off out of this shithole."

The man reappeared from behind the partition and handed Ozzie a bundle of paper. It contained a pita bread filled with long, coiled shavings of cooked meat.

Normally, kebab meat would be brown, and carved fresh from the slab before the customer. However, neither Finn nor Mick were in any condition to notice that this meat was grey with flecks of pale pink and had been handed to Ozzie from the back of the shop.

"Do you want chilli and salad?"

Mick's frown and the grimace on his lips told Ozzie all he needed to know. Extra chilli, extra onions, and no lettuce. He smiled as poured the hot sauce over the meat, then added lettuce, onions, tomatoes, and cucumber. He did exactly the same to Finn's.

"That will be eight pounds, please," Ozzie said politely.

Mick smashed a ten-pound note on the counter. "Keep the change," he sneered. "You look like you fucking need it."

As the two laughing men staggered out of the shop with their neatly wrapped bundles of meat, the old man came back from behind the counter. He leaned and watched as Mick and Finn walked up the dark, wet street. He turned to Ozzie and began to chatter. The younger man shrugged as he listened, nodding every now and then. Eventually, the older man threw his hands in the air and returned behind the partition. Ozzie stayed in the front of the shop, watching through the window as the two men unwrapped and began to eat their meals in the shelter of a bus stop. He grinned as he watched them.

CHAPTER
—2—

The stink waffed through the whole of the house. It crept down the stairs like a predator stalking it prey, spreading itself into every room, into every corner, into every nook and cranny. It was thick, so thick it almost had a physical presence. It was cloying, like an old chip pan that hadn't had the fat changed for months, but it was also sweet, like the sickly sweetness of rotting flesh left out in the elements for far too long.

The sounds were almost as bad as the smell. For every single heave and retch, there was another sound, this one long, rasping… and wet. It added to the stink in a more personal way. This was a human smell, almost too human.

Finn was bent over the toilet.

His fingers were almost white as they grasped the filthy rim of the bowl. His pale, wet head pushed further inside the porcelain maw with each heave. He retched again. This time with so much force he thought his eyes might bulge right out of their sockets and fall into the yellow jelly-like content before him. The thought of pushing his hands deep into the warm mixture of bile, half-digested meat, and other stuff he couldn't recognise made him heave again. With this heave came another long, hissing, moist escape from the other end of his body. With this release came more of the sugary, beige stink.

A chunk of… something… fell from his nose, splatting onto the ugly mixture in the bowl and resting like a film of oil on the surface of the toilet water. The splash from the gelatinous liquid him hit him in the face, turning his stomach again.

It was the stink that was making him feel worse after each heave. He wanted to pull his head out of the grime encrusted toilet, but he knew he couldn't. Every time he moved his head, he felt his brain move with it only half a second later. The ugly feeling of vertigo and nausea combined, causing his stomach to flip again, and no matter how much he had already vomited, no matter how empty his stomach was, it seemed he had more and more in reserve ready to expel. All he could see was a vista of vomit, regurgitated kebab, and thin skid marks of stuff he couldn't even identify clinging to the sides of the porcelain and—impossibly, he thought—ingrained into the underside of the rim.

Add to all of this the sickly-sweet pungent of what he affectionately knew as "Ale farts," and Finn was having a fucking party.

The worst party he'd ever attended in his life.

His stomach was cramping, his bowels were evacuating, his head was throbbing against his skull, he was freezing cold but also sweating at the same time.

As he wished for death to burst through the window—or even out of the toilet itself, covered in absolutely everything his body could afford to lose—and take his soul, he promised himself that he was never, ever drinking again.

It was a prophetic promise.

***

Mary was at the bathroom door. She was still in her pyjamas, and her hair was tousled with the madness that spoke of a restless, sleepless night. She had a thick woolly bed sock covering her mouth and nose. It was bravely standing up against the onslaught, the barrage of vileness that was coming at her with wave after relentless wave of filth in the air. Her head was shaking as she witnessed with wide, stinging eyes the sideshow spectacle that was her husband. He was kneeling on the cold floor with his back to her. A wet, dark stain had settled into the crease of his tight underwear. It had leaked from the confines of the stretched material and was now dripping down his legs, pooling on the expensive white vinyl tiles of the bathroom floor. The ones she had been so proud of. *Well, they're pretty much fucked now,* she fumed. She would have said it aloud but didn't dare remove the sock.

Finn took another heave, shouting violent, incomprehensible prayers to the Great Lord Huey who lived down the pan. She'd watched him worship Huey before, many times. *Too many times,* she thought, but it had never been like this.

He had never shit himself before.

Well, not since we were kids, she thought, shivering at the thought of the time they had hired a caravan when they had been still courting.

Her forehead creased with every heave. She didn't want it to, she wanted to be worried about him, to go to him and try to help him feel better, but her anger at the situation wouldn't allow her.

He'd come in last night soaking wet, stinking of ale, piss, and some cheap, shitty kebab. She'd listened to him piss all over the bathroom floor and fall all over the room as he tried to take his clothes off before eventually falling into the bed. He'd turned around to her, breathing what she could only imagine death smelt like into her face, and tried to instigate sex.

He nudged her, snuggling his reeking breath into her neck, fumbling at her breast, and urging her to "Come on, you used to love it after a drink." He had been relentless, pushing his fun-sized chocolate bar, semi-erect penis into her back. Eventually, she relented, just to get some peace, and attempted to give him a hand-job to keep him quiet, but his cock was like playdoh in her hands, refusing to go hard.

The words to an old song sprang to her mind. *The spirit is willing, but the flesh, it was weak.* This had made her laugh a little before she had to give up as her hand was cramping.

It didn't even matter because he was already asleep on his back with his dick still in her hand. She shook her head and released the beaten, flaccid thing from her grip.

As she went into the bathroom to wash her hands, the snoring started.

The snoring that woke the kids.

Seething, she resigned herself to climbing into bed with one of the boys.

"What's that noise, Mummy?" Tommy whispered as he moved over, allowing her to enjoy the warmth her son had created.

"It's nothing, baby. Just Daddy has an upset stomach, that's all. Go to sleep now," she soothed, as they both drifted off into the worst sleep she had attempted in years.

CHAPTER
—3—

"**W**hat the fuck is going on, Finn?" she asked, the annoyance in her voice more than evident. "Are you going to be long? I've got to do my makeup before I get the kids up. You've stunk the whole house out all night. It's out of order. Some of us have work, you know."

He lifted his head from out of the bowl and looked up at her.

What she saw disgusted her.

His eyes were pink, almost red. His skin was so pale it was almost green. She had never seen anyone physically turn green before. "Jesus Christ! How much did you drink last night?"

Finn swallowed; she could see it hurt him to do so and was just a little bit glad about it. He then wiped the dirty, yellowing water that was dripping from his chin.

"Not that much," he croaked. "Mick had to go home early, so we only had a few."

"Well, that's a load of shit, for a start," she hissed, resigning herself to doing her makeup in the bedroom. "You were done in when you got home, and whatever muck you'd eaten is all down your shirt. You're going to have to iron yourself a clean one for work today. I haven't got time... or, quite frankly, the fucking inclination."

At the mention of work, Finn turned away from her and another chunk of vomit hit the rest of what was already in the bowl.

"And don't think I'm cleaning that out either. I know you, you dirty bastard. The bleach is under the sink..." she shouted, making her way back towards the kids' rooms, where the first signs of them waking up could be heard. "I'm going to take the kids for a shitty fast-food breakfast. I'm not having them eating in this... squalor!"

***

"It's not a hangover, I've caught something. I think It's a bug," Finn lied again as he held the phone in his wet grip against his face. He was relishing the cool of the damp glass against his skin.

"You don't fool me, Finnley," the female voice on the other end of the line snapped. As she did, the tinny, electronic voice pierced his ear, making his head spin, like the rides in the fairgrounds he loved so much in his youth. "You sound hungover to me. This is the..." he heard papers being shuffled and shook his head, instantly regretting the action as it made his stomach churn again. "...fourth time this year you have taken a single day off, for a *bug*." The last word was spoken as if it was a dirty word.

"I'll prove it. I'll put you on video phone. You'll see how bad I am." It hurt his head and throat to talk, but if he wanted to keep his job, he knew he was going to have to keep going.

"No, that won't be—"

Finn had already activated the video call, and the image of the bookish, middle-aged woman who was his boss came alive on his screen.

"Holy Jesus," she uttered as she saw how he looked.

"This is no hangover," he pleaded his case.

He could feel the nasty chemical reaction that had been tearing his stomach apart all morning happen again. The delayed reaction and spinning of his brain, the churning of his stomach, the cramps, the weakened, aching legs—all of these symptoms combined, creating a perfect storm in his belly as the conversation with his boss continued.

"Listen, I've... I've got to go... ugh, right now," he gulped, half whispering as he swallowed thick saliva that had materialised in his mouth. The acidic taste of the saliva was the last straw, and he heaved.

He closed his mouth, not wanting to do this here in the hallway, but his body had other ideas. It needed to expel whatever was poisoning him, and if it couldn't make it out of his mouth, it would just find another way.

Warm, lumpy vomit exploded from his nostrils. He couldn't catch a breath and had to open his mouth. As he did, the same spray came from there. It covered his hand in wet warmth. It also covered the phone. Thick clumps of old meat and other *stuff* dripped down the glass, clinging into the creases of the plastic case he used on the device.

I'll never get all of that out, he thought before he looked at the screen. In between the dripping, foul liquid, he could see the face of Jane Bower. She looked to be gagging herself at what she had just witnessed on her screen.

He clicked the red button on his phone screen, ignoring the ugly sounds from his line manager, and ran, or whatever his body allowed him to do, up the stairs. He barely made it to the bathroom before another sour spray burst from his mouth and streamed from his nose.

As he fell to his knees, thrusting his head into the abhorrent toilet bowl, heaving, something inside him gave way. The ball of agony in his stomach deflated, only slightly, as his body sent a large portion of the poison it was trying to expel the other way.

As the pressure from his stomach subsided, he felt the slop dribbling from his backside, soiling the housecoat he was wearing. He wanted to cry but knew that no amount of tears would clean up the mess he had just left behind him on the new tiles, or the mess in the hallway.

He closed his eyes, enjoying the reprieve from the sickness that had plagued him all last night and all morning. The relief was short lived as the sweet smell of the newly arrived waste wafted up his nostrils, turning his stomach again, and a new flow of chunder flew from his mouth.

Eventually, the fit passed, and he was able to relax his burning face against the cool bowl. As the porcelain cooled his flesh, he took the moment to evaluate his life. He had shit himself, vomited over his boss during a video conversation, and hurled all over the hallway. He saw this as a spectacular low in an ever-expanding series of lows.

He pulled himself up, his hands slipping on the wet bowl a couple of times, and he coughed. As he did, a chunk of something soft dislodged from somewhere that was either the back of his throat or his nose; either way, it turned his stomach again and began another round of retch-o-rama.

In between the throbbing behind his eyes, his wayward brain, and his tumultuous stomach, he managed to marvel at how much *stuff* his stomach held.

When he stopped again, he held his breath, willing himself to stop being sick. He reached down to his waist and struggled to untie the belt of his shit-dripping housecoat. He braved standing up, even though he didn't trust his legs, and managed to remove the heavy, cold garment. He held it out at a shaky arm's length before dropping it into the shower without so much as looking at it. He knew that if he did, it would start him up all over again. He then removed his soiled underpants. As he flung them, he caught sight of a couple of rogue splashes flying across the room, coating two of the toothbrushes in the glass above the sink.

"Fuck!" was all he could bring himself to croak about that.

He made a mental note to remember to remove the toothbrushes just as soon as he could get his body to stop rebelling against him and he was able deal with such a shitty situation. He knew that wouldn't be for hours, at least.

With his head still reeling, his vision doubling and blurring, he managed to grab a towel from the back of the door. It was moist. He didn't know who had used it last, and he didn't care. He wiped his face with it, smearing the greasy sweat and the vomit from his face. He then used it to mop up the mess on the floor. It was hard work as he still couldn't bring himself to look at it. He then turned on the shower.

With his legs still unsteady, he watched the beige water stream from the towels, the underwear, and the housecoat. It was racing towards the plug hole, a brown tide of frothing filth, littered with unidentifiable clumps—and some he thought he could identify.

It was meat!

More specifically, it was kebab meat.

It was grey.

The brown had washed out of it, probably from his stomach acid and the water from the shower. Even though the chunk was mesmerising as it twisted and turned in the dirty water, heading towards the oblivion of the plughole, he had to pull his eyes from it. Just focusing on it was making him dizzy.

Dizzy meant vomiting again, and he didn't want to do that.

He breathed deep of the steam. It was a shaky breath, and the smell was still horrendous, but it cleared some of the more bitter-tasting morsels still residing in the tubes of his throat and nose. He hocked up more thickness and spat it into the toilet. It surprised him that this didn't induce another bout of vomiting. He took encouragement from it. *Maybe I'm over the worst,* he thought, but he wasn't entirely convinced of that yet.

Carefully, he stepped into the hot, steaming water, allowing it to cascade over his body, lowering his head so it could run through his hair and down his face. He'd expected to feel better about himself as the water cleaned off the stinking sweat, the drying vomit, and the shit from his skin, but he didn't. Each drip of water felt like a pin piercing his skin, slicing him into ribbons. *Death by a million cuts,* he thought, wanting to smile but physically not able to do so. He lifted his head so the water could run over his face, hoping for some, even if it was only minuscule, relief. Just a small break from the Hell he was experiencing; but it wasn't forthcoming.

If anything, he felt worse.

"Never again," he whispered, allowing the hot water to fill his mouth. "Never, ever, again!"

Shivering, not from the cold, because it wasn't, but from the physical exertions his body had been put through, he stepped out of the shower and bent down to pick his towel from the floor.

It was cold and heavier than it should have been, but before his fevered brain could put two and two together, he rubbed his wet face with it.

That was when he realised why it was cold.

He opened his eyes and looked at it, at what it was covered in, and what was now covering his face and hands. An involuntary gag rose from his stomach. The exertion of this retch started his brain back into a spinning cycle, and before he knew it, his nose was back, inches from the filth he'd vomited earlier as he buried his face deep into the toilet bowl.

Why didn't I flush? he sobbed to himself between hurls.

His stomach was cramping badly now. It felt like when he used to go to the gym, back when he was a boy, and he and Mick would have competitions to see who could do the most sit-ups.

When that excruciating agony passed, he sat back onto the stained floor and breathed deep. His whole world stunk of nothing else but shit. Not the diluted smell of a gassy fart, this was thick, undulating, repellent. It was his whole world right now. He had never, ever found himself in a situation like this. He'd had hangovers in the past, but this was something else.

Am I dying? he thought, wondering exactly how much his body could take before he'd die. He must have emptied his stomach by now, but it was more than obvious he hadn't.

The stink over his face and hands wracked his stomach with more nausea. He used his weakened arms and faeces-greased hands to lift himself onto his unsteady legs, using the toilet for leverage. He reached for the flush, wanting to rid the bowl of what was in there before it caused a biohazard.

Everywhere he touched, he left a smudge. It was disgusting, but so was he, so was his whole world, his very essence was fucking disgusting.

As he pushed the lever, he caught a glimpse of himself in the shaving mirror. He didn't like what he saw, not one bit. He'd heard the saying "Green behind the gills" before but never, ever thought he would witness it in the first person.

His skin, the bits he could see between the smudged shit, was green. It wasn't a cool Hulk green, or even a sexy green like the girls on *Star Trek* that he'd beaten himself off to when he was a kid. This was a sickly, rotting green, like something out of a cheap zombie film.

The hollows of his eyes and nose were the worst. A rash had formed on his cheeks and across his forehead. It made the mawkish discolouration look even worse in contrast. He took in a slow, shaky breath, loosening more lumps of vomit still languishing in his tubes, and spat them out, grimacing at their bitterness. He waited in grim anticipation of his stomach turning and restarting the whole process...

It was a small mercy that it didn't happen.

He ran the water in the sink and rinsed the shit from his face, taking note of how badly his hands were shaking. "What the fuck was in those pints last night?" He sighed; his voice was as unsteady as his hands.

He looked that the sopping wet, soiled underwear in the shower and the sodden, sullied towel on the floor, and shook his head.

Taking baby steps and reaching for anything and everything that might help him, he escaped from the bathroom, towards the bedroom. He opened a drawer, hoping to find some clean underwear but only finding a vest, then climbed, bottomless, onto the bed, hoping not to unsettle anything that might still be residing in his stomach, before exhaling another shaky sigh.

He closed his eyes. He wanted to welcome sleep, to allow it to whisk him away from the damnation where he currently dwelled, maybe even taking him forever, to sleep the eternal sleep of the people who had just given up.

Both sounded equally inviting.

He had no recollection of it, but he must have fallen asleep.

He opened his eyes, and the room and everything around him was dark. Panic gripped him as he thought that either his wish to die had been granted or his eyesight had failed. Then he saw the small clock on the bedside table, and relief washed over him. The numbers swam before eventually coming together and sliding into a fuzzy focus.

It was almost six p.m.

He opened both eyes and swallowed. He lay as still as he could, assessing the situation. Miraculously, there was no pain, and the room wasn't spinning. *It's gone,* he thought. *Thank fuck for that, the hangover's gone!*

His body jumped as the front door slammed. He could feel his sickly heart hammering in his chest, yet he welcomed the rush of adrenaline it sent though his ruined corpse. The sounds of his wife entering the house filtered up from the hallway.

He assumed she was taking her shoes off.

"What the fuck is that stink?" she shouted as he heard her footsteps starting up the stairs. She stopped after only a few steps. "Jesus Christ, it smells like something's died up there. You're a dirty bastard, Finnley. It fucking stinks like an abattoir."

Like you know what an abattoir smells like, he thought, attempting a smile but not quite able to complete it. Then he remembered, with a sudden panic, the housecoat and his underpants were still in the shower, and the towel, it was still on the floor covered in shit. He sat up, swinging his feet off the bed. It was just a small movement, an attempt to get out of bed, to head her off, to get into the bathroom before she could. It seemed that the hangover had not had the last of him just yet. His head began to spin again as his life came crashing back down around him.

The ceiling was up, then it was almost next to his face, then it was beneath him. The walls were undulating, breathing in and out, in and out. The floor was a sea of jelly. His feet couldn't find any purchase, any solidity to support his weight.

His legs were spaghetti. Not the straight, dried spaghetti but perfectly cooked sticks of pasta; he couldn't control them, and even if he could, he didn't think he had any bones inside them to use. His shoulders and arms were suddenly lead weights, and before he knew it, something hit him full in the face.

It was the floor. The jelly had gone, and it was suddenly solid again.

Too solid.

His brain didn't register the crunch of his nose until at least two seconds after the rest of his body had. The dizziness mixed with the unexpected inertia flipped his stomach again. His mouth opened and his stomach cramped. Thick, bitter yellow liquid oozed from between his lips. It pooled on the carpet around his chin. It smelt caustic, causing him to retch... again.

The difference now, there was nothing left in his stomach to expel. All that came forth was hot, stinging, sour bile. Surely, it had to be the last of it. The disgusting vile scum that had been residing at the pit of his stomach.

It was all becoming too much to bear.

"Finn? Finn are you OK?" Mary shouted as he heard the thumping of her feet on the stairs. "Finn, what was that noise? Are you OK?"

He wanted to answer but couldn't.

As he lay face down on the floor, his nose throbbing in time with his head, he had nothing left. He was drained, there was not even enough energy to speak.

"Jesus Christ, Finn. What the hell were you drinking last night?" she snapped as she popped her head into the bedroom, covering her nose with her blouse. "It smells like a sewer! Have you shit yourself?"

Finn's eyes rolled towards her, and a small drip of yellow drool slid from his mouth, staining the beige carpet beneath him.

He needed to stop her from entering the bathroom. He knew it would all blow up, big time, once she saw the mess in there, but he couldn't move. There wasn't enough oomph in him to even move his arms, never mind get up and stop her.

"I'm sorry," he mumbled, as he heard her sharp intake of breath. "I'm so sorry!"

"Jesus Christ! You are a fucking disgrace, Finnley James! You're an animal, worse than an animal. If you think I'm cleaning that up, you've got another thing coming," she shouted, storming back down the stairs. "I'm not going anywhere near *that!*"

He could hear her talking to the kids; her voice was hushed, theirs were not.

"What's that stink?" Kyle, their son, whined.

"Has Daddy had an accident?" Tommy asked in the same voice.

Summoning every bit of strength he had, he pushed himself off the floor and into an upright sitting position. His arms were heavy and unresponsive, and it zapped him of energy just moving them. *What is wrong with me?* he thought, trying to ignore the spinning in his head.

He needed to get to the bathroom. He needed to clean up the mess he'd left in there, for Mary, but mostly so the kids didn't see it. However, his legs were not playing the same game as his brain; they flatly refused to work as they should. His knees were stiff, and his calves felt swollen. He looked down at himself and was surprised to see a pink rash on his inner thigh. In the whole scheme of things, it was nothing that concerned him, but he didn't remember it being there earlier.

He looked up at his bed, but even the minute shifting of his head was too much for his overly delicate stomach, and he felt the now familiar gorge of vomit twisting in his stomach. He imagined it like the window of a washing machine. Bile, undigested food, and other intestinal fluids spinning and spinning and spinning. More stinging vomit dribbled from his mouth. It spilled down his chin, down his already discoloured vest, and pooled into a warm, frothy lagoon in his crotch.

He sobbed. Mary was going to kill him, but right now, that didn't matter. He needed to climb back into the bed. He would deal with whatever fall-out would come tomorrow. As the bile cooled in his lap, dripping onto the already stained and, he had to face facts, ruined carpet, he began to cry. Real tears flowed from his eyes as his face screwed itself up into a grimace. He didn't know how long it had been since the last time he had cried, and it shocked him to learn that he didn't know how to do it properly. He tried, he wanted to, but each time he did, it felt fake.

He swallowed, tasting the bitterness of the residue of vomit in his mouth, and heaved himself up off the floor. It took so much effort to stand up that all he could do was crawl onto the bed. He leaned over and grabbed the metal wastepaper bin, taking it with him. He had an idea he was going to need it during the night.

***

At some point, he heard Mary come into the room.

Although not one-hundred-percent sure of anything at that point, he thought he heard her gag and close the door again.

He heard her going into another room in the house and closing the door.

He was going to either get hell or the silent treatment in the morning, but right now he didn't care. He needed sleep, he needed to rest, and he needed the washing machine combination of his head and stomach to stop spinning.

Mick had not stopped vomiting all day. His wife had been out working her two jobs to help keep the roof over their heads while he had told her he was working from home.

Every single time he moved, he vomited. His head was spinning, his stomach was churning, and his legs were like jelly. After seven hours of this, he had managed to keep down some tablets and was now feeling a little more human than he had that morning when Paula left for work.

It was a blessing that they had no children. He had never had the appetite for them or, to be honest, the time for them. All he wanted was his wife to cook and clean for him and allow him to do what he wanted in the bedroom.

Basically, he wanted a slave, a domestic and a sexual one.

And unwitting or not, Paula had become one.

From early in their relationship, he had manipulated her, beaten her, told her he would kill her, then her family, and finally himself if she ever left him.

She never did.

The beatings never stopped and neither did the bullying. It was almost as if she enjoyed it.

He didn't know if he was kidding himself or if he *was* feeling better, but the last thing he wanted to do was show her any weakness when she got home. She needed to know that her man, her caveman husband, was fit and healthy.

I won't be like that little weed, Finn. Always snivelling to his cunt of wife, he thought, smiling even though it hurt his face to do so. Almost every time they were out together and his phone went off, Finn would jump. He would cow to that bitch, like a bitch himself.

He laughed, and it hurt. It really hurt, and it made him lose his breath. Aside from the incessant banging of his head and the churning of his stomach, which the tablets he had managed to keep down were trying their best to sort, he was only really worried about the nasty little rash he had found within the crease of his groin.

His balls had been itchy, ragingly so, and he'd been raking at them with his fingers all morning. He only stopped when a thick layer of flesh peeled away from them. Then he stopped scratching instantly. He didn't want to look down, as every time he moved his head, it caused him to vomit, but also, he didn't really want to see what he had just done to one of the most precious parts of his body. He passed the flesh between his fingers, only guessing what it could be. There was no pain coming from his sack, and he couldn't feel any blood flowing.

He braved a quick look. It took a moment for his vision to focus, and he was glad he was already lying down as he might have fallen at that point. There was a long strip of skin in his fingers, some of it caught behind the fingernail of his index finger. As he looked at it, his head began to swim again, and his stomach churned. For some reason, one he couldn't fathom, he sniffed the browny-pink strip of flesh.

It smelt like cold kebab meat.

He didn't know if it was his fingers that smelt like that or if it was the skin, but either way, his mouth filled with water, and he knew he was going to throw up.

He did.

It was only a little bit of sick, and he managed to catch it in his mouth. It was warm, and it was lumpy, but as he didn't want to admit weakness to himself, he closed his eyes and swallowed it, clumps and all. The taste was revolting. It was so sour and bitter, it stung his throat as the thickness slid down his gullet, back into the stomach from where it had just been expelled. His grimace turned into a shiver as regurgitation threatened to give it another appearance.

By breathing deeply through his nose, he just about managed to control it, and he stemmed the vomit.

Looking down at the offending piece of skin, he shivered again. It was too thick and too brown for it to be fresh. It looked old, like it had flaked off the body of a corpse or something. A horrible thought occurred that he has split his ball-sack right open and his testicles could be lolling all over the bed, only attached to him by thin tubes. Frantically, he looked down at his crotch and lifted his scrotum. He breathed a sigh of relief when he saw it was still attached to his body. Yet, he needed to see where the strip of flesh had come from. He wasn't feeling any pain down there, but he needed to be sure.

As he felt around, a sharp stinging sensation forced him into a quick, sharp intake of breath. His fingers had found the wet strip, the sore part. He hoped it might have just been a bit of scratch-rash from some overzealous itching, but it felt worse than that. It felt like he'd torn his skin. He looked at his fingers; this time there was blood, not much, but enough to turn his stomach again.

He didn't like the thought of his balls bleeding, not one bit.

Ignoring the fuzziness in his head and stomach, he pulled his underpants back up and made his way to the toilet. He needed to relieve himself, *and maybe get some more tablets.* He looked at the clock, it was almost six p.m. He'd wasted the day feeling like shit and vomiting.

He exhaled a hefty sigh as he removed his penis from his underwear, ready to release a hot stream, then he noticed something on the tip. It was something he hadn't seen for years, not since he was in his teenage years.

It was a thick, white lining, underneath and protruding from his foreskin.

He frowned. There was a distinct smell wafting up from it. It was familiar somehow, but not one he would have associated or remembered with dick cheese. He inserted a finger underneath the excess skin around his dick and ran it around, collecting whatever discharge had built in there.

Once again, curiosity go the better of him, and despite his fuzzy head and delicate stomach, he sniffed his slime coated finger.

He recalled and expected the stink of blue cheese. He even smiled at a memory of chasing the girls around the gym in school with it on his finger. *Huh, wouldn't be able to do that in these* sensitive *days,* he thought with a scoff.

But it wasn't cheese he smelled.

It was cooked meat. Like fried bacon that had been left to go cold. Or fast-food burger that had been left overnight.

His stomach was about to flip again when he heard a noise from downstairs.

"Mick, I'm home," Paula shouted up the stairs, the levity in her voice already grating on his fuzzy brain.

He looked at the white build-up on his finger one more time before flicking it into the bowl. He then allowed his pee to flow.

It stung.

It seemed hotter than usual, and as he grimaced, he pulled his foreskin back over the tip of his cock. A rogue squirt of pee flew from his slit and splashed onto the back of the toilet, all over the seat.

He looked at the piss.

For fucks sake, he thought as an anger descended over him. *What now?*

Feeling dizzy, he bent down to get a better look at the pee. It was thick, *Probably why it stung so much.* But it wasn't the consistency of it that had caught his eye.

It was the colour.

It was a dark yellow, almost green. It looked like something that he would have coughed up if he had a bad cold or the man-flu. There was something else in there too.

That something else, something he was sure was blood.

"Mick, are you up there?" Paula shouted, making her way up the stairs.

Slag! was the only thought running through his head. *Fucking slag. She's obviously been putting it around a bit. I bet It's that prick from her office, and now I'm infected with her dirty shit.*

With a pink mist clouding his vision, ironically making him feel better than he had all day, he took two tablets from the mirrored cupboard and swallowed them with a splash of water. The anger was doing wonders. It cleared his head, taking away the consistent throb, and the adrenaline coursing through his body was doing miracles for his upset stomach.

"I'm in the bathroom," he replied, his voice light despite the anger raging through him. He splashed water on his face and looked at himself in the mirror, breathing deeply and watching the water drip from his chin. He didn't care that it was off colour as it dripped into the sink—white, milky, greasy.

Fucking whore! If she's given me something, I'm going to make her pay for it.

"Are you OK? Fuck's sake, Mike. It stinks in here. Have you been cooking?"

Cooking? He asked himself. *What fucking planet is this woman on?* He took a few deep breaths and splashed more water on his face; he wanted to be on his game for this.

"No, baby," he called from the bathroom. "I just wanted to take a shower."

He had no intention of taking a shower. He knew he stunk and that his dick had that filthy grime around the tip; he wanted her to get the full effect of the infection she had so obviously passed on to him.

"A shower? What's the special occasion?" she laughed.

"Aw, nothing. It's just that I was so drunk when I came in last night, I wanted to make it up to you, that's all."

"Ooh, make it up me?" she asked, her voice rising a few octaves.

He stepped out of the bathroom, naked and ready for business. "Yeah, make it up to you. So, you know," he shrugged, gesturing first towards his hard-on, and then the bedroom. "Let's go in here and I'll make it up to you."

Her eyes roamed over his body, lingering for an extra moment on his erection. Her expression was one of defeat. Her shoulders sagged, and all the joy went out of her face.

He grinned. He loved it when she rolled over for him to tickle her belly.

"Mick, I've only just got in," she protested. "I'll have to make the dinner, get a shower."

He looked at her. His whole body was weak, shaky, otherworldly, but he was determined to not show her any of this. He was strong, determined to do with her what he wanted. If she was going around spreading her whore legs for all and sundry, then he was going to give her a taste of her own medicine.

Literally... a taste!

With her head bowed, she walked past him and his erection, entering the dark bedroom. "Christ!" she exclaimed. "What have you been doing in here?" She gagged, holding her nose. "It fucking stinks."

As if in an attempt to answer her question, he grabbed her hair, pushing her head into the sheets of the unmade bed. At first, she protested, but not much. She couldn't, as before she could wriggle free, he had twisted her arm behind her back, while his other hand fumbled at her panties, having already lifted her skirt.

The fight in her dissipated rather rapidly, and she became the complacent little lamb he loved so much. *Just the way I like it.* He grinned, spitting on his hand. He was annoyed at the thick saliva he produced; his throat was almost bone dry, but it would do the trick. He rubbed his glue-like spit between her legs, then pulled her head back by her hair and whispered into her ear. "This the way you like it, isn't it?"

"You fucking know it is..." she whispered back.

He plunged his fingers into her mouth, and she sucked the spit and her juices off them, moaning as she did. He pulled her head harder, tighter, exposing her neck. Letting go of her arm, he wrapped his hand around her vulnerable throat.

"Have you been fucking that prick in your office again?" he hissed into her ear.

She tried to answer, but her head was too far back, and all she could do was cough a little and struggle for breath. He relented his hold on her.

"You know I have," she croaked, a line of drool dripping from her mouth onto his sopping fingers.

"Is that right, eh?"

"Fuck, yeah."

"Is his dick bigger than mine?" he whispered, tightening his grip around her neck.

She sighed and wiggled her arse, pushing it back towards his rock-solid dick. "Bigger and thicker," she replied, giggling.

"Is that so?" he asked. "Does it make you feel like... this?" He plunged his dick deep into her welcoming gash, and she gasped as he pushed it in. "Does it?" he asked again, this time spitting it through gritted teeth.

"You know it doesn't," she whined.

He liked it when she whined.

He spat on his hand again and pushed it into her face, she lapped at the thick spit hungrily as he pushed his cock inside her, deeper and deeper. He slapped her ass cheeks with each thrust, not holding back on the power behind the hits. He loved watching her skin turn from olive to pink, then red, and eventually to deep purple as the bruises began to form.

Normally, when doing it like this, he was fast to get to the point of no return. Today was no different. The tell-tale signs that he was near had begun. The familiar tingle in his feet followed by the itch in the base of his cock.

Only this time, it felt different.

The itch in his cock wasn't its normal, playful little tickle. It stung. There was a sharp pain in his balls and in the base of his shaft.

No, something wasn't right. It felt like something was pushing its way up his dick, trying to get out. Which, of course it was. He continued to thrust into her, deeper, almost making her cry, until it was time to bring it all to an end.

"Turn over, you fucking whore," he ordered, more than a little out of breath and his head spinning. He'd had a bad day, he was tired, and he still felt sick. Yet he was unrelenting in what he wanted to do to his bitch. It excited him more and more with the things she allowed him, enjoyed him doing to her.

Without protest, she turned over and lay on the edge of the bed. She opened her mouth, inviting him in to finish.

He stood over her, straddling her head, enjoying the feeling of her fingers climbing up his inner thighs. He knew they were going towards his arsehole, and he allowed them to venture there. He loved nothing more than receiving two fingers up his hoop as he shot his load over her face. He shuffled forwards, his hands stroking the length of his shaft, bending slightly, giving her easier access to his chute. He grabbed at one of her tits as he felt her fingers slide inside him. He grinned as he remembered he'd had the runs earlier, damn near shit himself when he was puking into the toilet. He liked the idea of her hands getting dirty.

It seemed she didn't mind either.

As he continued to wank into her face, he noticed her pulling a small face. Just a wrinkle of her nose as he rubbed his pre-cum over her nose. She never usually grimaced like that, she usually attempted to lick it, wanting to get as much of his juices into her mouth as she could. She protested a little as he pushed his cock deep into her open mouth.

As he pulled it out, she coughed. A thick white bridge of spit spanned from her lips to the head of his cock.

"Fucking hell, Mick. Where's that thing been?" she gasped. "It tastes—"

He didn't allow her to finish her sentence; he was eager to get to the finish line.

The pain and the pressure in his cock was intense. The usual euphoria he felt right before cumming, especially into her mouth, was ruined. His dick felt like it was about to explode. The pressure surging up from the inside was almost too much to bear. Whatever was coming forth was not like anything that had ever come before. It felt thick and too much for his shaft to accommodate. It was like trying to push a football through a hosepipe.

He pushed her back onto the bed and straddled her face, allowing his balls to dangle into her mouth.

While licking his grease coated balls, she slid her finger back into his hole, knuckle deep, and began to twirl it around and around. It wasn't having its usual effect. Usually this caused him to explode, to cover her forehead, mouth, and chin in his larger than usual spray. He liked to hold her nose too, so she would choke on his cum; he enjoyed the way her face flushed almost purple as her windpipe blocked.

But today, it wasn't as pleasurable as normal. Today, it just felt like she was dislodging something inside him.

The agony of what was happening caused him to scream. He looked down as he continued to massage his length. He looked at Paula, lying underneath him with her mouth open, ready to accept his load. The only thing was, he didn't know what it was he was about to unload.

Her fingers were still probing his arse when his stomach clenched.

With a roar of pain, he came.

Thick, yellowy... what was it? He didn't know. But he did know it wasn't cum. It looked like grease to him, like the old fat in a chip-pan, complete with little black bits. It exploded from the tip of his cock into Paula's mouth.

His legs buckled and his chest heaved. He thought he was about to have a heart attack as the thick, vile-smelling substance *birthed* from his manhood.

He remembered a cartoon he'd watched once, where a small, angry red-haired man had been hunting a large grey rabbit. The rabbit had loaded too much shot into the man's gun, and when he pulled the tigger, the gun exploded, the barrel of the rifle ribboning into four crumpled metal shards.

That was what he felt his penis was going to look like.

Then his stomach let go of his cramp. Paula's fingers were still in his rectum. Only he could feel damage happening up there. It was no longer fun.

With another orgasmic scream, his stomach let go.

He couldn't help it. It just happened.

Hot, stinging slurry poured from out of his sphincter. It made his eyes water as it left him, adding to the stinging he was feeling in his still erect cock.

He shit all over Paula's face.

He hadn't meant to, he had never done it before, but he couldn't stop.

He could hear her gagging below him, gagging with her mouth closed. She pulled her fingers out of him, but this just added to the exodus, widening his hole and allowing more sludge to escape.

He had nothing left in him, and he fell forwards, his face hitting her stomach. Normally, he would spend a few minutes going down on her in his favourite sixty-nine position, allowing her to swallow as much of his cum as she could while he got her off with his tongue, but not today.

Today, he felt as if he was about to die.

The thick sting of his greasy cum was, in its own way, as bad as the stink of his shit all over the bed and his wife's face.

She was wriggling beneath him, bucking him, trying to get him off her. He couldn't move. He didn't want to move. He just wanted to lie there and die in his own freaky expulsions.

"Jesus fucking Christ," Paula cursed, her voice plummy as she tried to keep her mouth closed. "Jesus fucking Christ," she bubbled, squirming out from beneath him.

Normally at this point, she would be swilling his load around her mouth, allowing it to dribble down her chin, mostly for show, for him, before swallowing the rest. This was not what she was doing now. She was bent over the side of the bed, rubbing at her face, retching like he'd been doing all day, and trying to scrape watery shit from her tongue.

"Christ, Mick. You know I like it rough," she said between gags as she covered a nostril and blew out of the other. A brown clump flew out. "But that's taking the fucking piss. I'm going to be smelling shit all day now. Besides, what the hell have you been eating?" she mumbled as she spat a thick globule of cum out of her mouth. Even though it was mixed with his faeces, it was still too thick and too yellow to be healthy cum. As it left her mouth, it looked like fat. The ugly fat that gathered around a cooked slab of meat. Brown, yellow, black, and greasy.

"You're a fucking pig," Paula uttered. "Don't you ever do that to me again, you hear me? I don't mind a bit of water sports, but fucking scat? I thought you were better than that."

He watched as a line of miscoloured drool hung from her mouth, almost all the way to the floor. There was grease and shit over her chin, splashed on her blouse. He was fascinated, mesmerised as the liquid shit and the grease from his cum refused to mix. He couldn't answer. He was suddenly freezing cold. He looked at the mess on the bed sheets wanting to apologise; he hadn't meant to do that to her, it had just happened.

Then there was a noise.

It sounded like a partially blocked drain ridding itself of trapped water, or the bath draining, only it was coming from his stomach.

His legs buckled again, and his knees bent.

The throbbing from his still-hard, misused penis was now nothing more than a mild inconvenience compared to what was occurring in his stomach. Something gripped inside. The noise came again, this time louder, more urgent. Paula, wiping her mouth from the mess he'd ejaculated all over her, looked up from spitting on the floor.

"Mick?"

It was all he heard her say before a grimace formed on his face and a howl of agony issued from him. He squatted, the pressure on his knees making them pop and moan, and his bowels opened up again.

Hot, clumpy firewater shot out from behind him, along with a long, gassy fart. The warmth was dripping down his legs, he could hear it hitting the carpet. The agony was immeasurable, it was off the charts. He felt like someone was inserting red hot pokers up his sphincter.

Someone was screaming his name, but it was so far away, so far in the foggy distance, that he paid it no mind. He was lost in a forest of pain, a universe of suffering.

The last thing he did was gag at the awful smell before his head splashed into a warm puddle of filth.

CHAPTER
—6—

"**W**hat is with those fucking birds," Finn growled. He opened his eyes, and the glare of light streaming through the window clawed at his eyes as the world slowly swam into focus around him. A large, untouched glass of water was sat on the bedside table, next to the clock, which read eight-thirty-two.

He was already late.

He was alone in the bed and thought that was only right, especially after the antics of yesterday.

He kicked the blankets off him, stretched, and jumped out of bed.

Or... at least that's what he tried to do.

In reality, he flapped at the covers, trying his utmost to flick the blankets that were his prison. However, he couldn't. This was for two reasons. The first was because his arms were not working as they normally should. It was like his bones were made of concrete. He guessed this might be because of the exertions his body went through yesterday having a detrimental effect on him.

The second reason he couldn't escape his material pokey was because it felt as though the sheets were stuck to him.

He was moist.

His whole body felt damp; cold and wet.

Please, please don't tell me I've shit the bed!

A small wriggle of his torso told him he hadn't. It was only a small reprieve.

The whole room was unpleasant. There was a stink, like a chip pan that had been left uncovered for a few weeks and the fat had gone hard and bad. He lifted his head, only slightly, just to test if the bad effects from the day and night before had abated. He was pleased to find out that the headache, dizziness, and nausea seemed to have diminished. They were not gone completely but were less pronounced than yesterday.

Worst day of my whole life, he thought, casting his mind back on the misadventures in the bathroom. By misadventures, he meant shitting himself, multiple times, on the floor, in front of his wife, *and possibly the kids.* This last thought caused him to wince more than the soreness of his arms, his neck, and his stomach combined.

As he released a shaky sigh, he smelt his own breath, and the vivid, disgusting memories of yesterday's filthy antics came flooding back to hit him around the head.

His neck was in agony.

He must have been lying funny and it needed clicking back into place. He tried to lift his arm to rub the back of his neck before remembering his limbs were stiff and sore. It took a lot of wincing coupled with a Herculean effort of sheer willpower to get his appendage where he needed it to go. When it finally got there, he began to rub his fingers into the sore spot, hoping to ease it back into some semblance of usefulness.

He grimaced at what he felt there. His skin was slick, almost oily.

He removed his hand, again with a lot of effort, and looked at it. There was a thin sheen of white covering the tips of his fingers.

He sniffed it.

His stomach rolled with the same familiar feelings as yesterday. It was the same stink as the room.

Old, sour fat.

With considerable effort, he wrestled the bed covers off him and looked down at his semi-naked body. It was covered in the same thin sheen. "What the fuck?" he mumbled through his dry mouth.

He prised himself up off the bed. The sheets stuck to his exposed flesh, and he had to fight to peel them off his chest and legs. Once free, he looked at his body, at the flesh beneath the white coating. His skin looked rough. There was a pink rash covering his upper thighs that crawled up towards his crotch, underneath his moist boxer shorts, and over his lower stomach. It was similar to the rash he'd noticed on his face yesterday.

He rubbed it. The feel of the mottled but soft skin beneath the thin, white layer of—*What? What the fuck is it?*—made him queasy. He wanted to shout Mary. He wanted her to come in, to sooth him, to tell him exactly what it was covering his body, but she would have already left for work by now, dropping the kids off on her way.

There was a wet sucking sound as he struggled to lift his heavy legs, peeling the blankets off them as he tried to ease himself off the bed.

His head swam as he sat up. It was bad, but it was nothing compared to what he had felt the day before. He put his hands on the duvet and pushed himself up, once again taking the sheets with him. He rolled his eyes and pulled them, along with his damp underwear, out of the crack of his behind.

As he stood up, the tingle of a sneeze was building in his nose. He held his breath, hoping it would pass, as he really didn't need the trauma of a sneeze right now, not in his fragile situation. However, the sneeze was persistent. It travelled down his nostrils, causing him to inhale a deep breath in readiness of the explosion.

The blast shook him to the core, as did the inevitable second one. He felt something thick fly from his nose and mouth.

He stumbled to the full-length mirror where the discharge from the sneeze had landed. Walking, even just the few feet to the mirror, felt strange to him, almost alien. Ignoring his reflection, or the reflection of the dead man in the glass—he didn't know, and didn't want to explore that, just yet—all his attention focused on the thick *stuff* that was sliding down the dark glass.

It was white.

It seemed to have the same consistency of what was covering his skin.

Carefully, he lifted his arm, reaching his hand out to touch it. He didn't know if the greasy smear was from the vile coating over his fingers or from whatever it was that had flown from his nose and mouth. Either way, it was disgusting.

He stepped back and studied his reflection. The room was dull, not quite dark, but his body stood out against what darkness there was, with the white sheen of—*of what?*—all over his skin. His hair was sticking up at strange angles, and he could see the stuff nestled in between the thinner parts of his hairline.

He licked his lip... and grimaced.

The taste of his skin was horrible.

He licked it again, coating the lining of his tongue. It felt like licking a cold pork chop.

He stepped back again and reached for the light switch. The infusion of the stark light pierced his eyeballs, and his reflection in the mirror blurred. The light reflected off the grotesque figure in the glass, and he squinted. He raised his hands, attempting to shield his eyes from the penetrating light as it stabbed into his brain. As his arms were far too heavy; all he managed to do was slap himself in the face, harder than he had expected. He staggered backwards, reaching out to grab the corner of the bed to stop himself from falling. As he did, his feet slipped from underneath him, and he fell anyway.

Sitting on the floor, he shook his head. If he didn't feel so much like shit, and wasn't covered in some horrible smelling grease, he might have laughed. However, laughter was a fair distance from where he was right now. He placed his hands on the floor to push himself back up, but they slipped, and he fell back again with a slap. He closed his eyes, took in a deep breath through his nostrils, and balked.

The stench from him was rank. "I will never, ever, eat another kebab again," he mumbled his prophetic declaration.

Looking past the ugly white film smothering his body, he noticed the rash had travelled up his legs, through his crotch and stomach, up his sides, and was now covering his neck. *What the fuck is that?* he pondered, shuffling closer to the glass surface. It was uglier on closer inspection. Running his fingers over it, he could feel how raised and mottled it was; it looked like old, burnt skin. His mind was taken back to those movies, his brain in such a fog that he couldn't even remember the name of them now. The one where the guy had knives for fingers—not scissors, that was a different film. He wore a hat and was plaguing teenagers' dreams.

A shiver ran through him as he turned away; he didn't want to see any more of it.

He realised he needed to go to the toilet. His bladder was screaming at him. He tried again to get up, his hands gripping the shag of the carpet to gain purchase, and eased himself up onto his feet. He looked down at where he'd been sitting and marvelled at the greasy stain he'd left on the carpet. He looked around the room and saw greasy footprints from the bed, and other stains where he'd puked and shit himself yesterday. *That's going to cost a fortune to replace,* he thought as he walked unsteadily across the room.

He trod in something nasty hiding in strands of the carpet.

He remembered bringing up bile last night; he also remembered not cleaning it up. He looked down at his foot and saw it immersed in a pool of something hideous. It was cold and jelly-like in substance, and there was a greasy film over the surface that his foot had broken.

He brought his foot up and marvelled at the thick slime clinging to his skin. It was like cheese on a hot pizza slice. He took another sigh as he made a mental note to clean it up after he'd been to the bathroom.

Standing over the bowl that he remembered—not very fondly—making love to yesterday was an odd feeling. He still felt queasy, nowhere near a hundred percent, but yesterday had been on another level. He swallowed the rising saliva in his mouth as he whispered an oath to the toilet, or to himself, he really didn't know which. "I'm *never* drinking again." It shocked him that his voice still had a waver to it. "Well, not in that pub anyway!"

He released himself from the confines of his sticky boxer shorts and grimaced when he saw the white filmy substance was covering the whole of his groin. His balls were shrivelled, and his penis had retracted into his body, leaving only a small nub of foreskin peeking timidly from the greasy mess of pubic hair between his legs.

Even though the rest of his body was covered in this slime, what was hanging from his foreskin was the worst of it.

It was a solid yellowing mass of God only knew what.

The thickness had pulled his foreskin back, and it was hanging out of his slit like hardened candle wax that had dried mid drip.

He had to look away. The very thought of it there, hanging from his dick like a stalactite from an old adventure movie, was too much. He creased his brow, wanting to cry as his fingers shakily pulled at the horrid protrusion. Almost like an iceberg, the bit he could see was only the tip. There was an odd but not entirely unpleasant sensation as he pulled the coagulated mass from of his cock. The longer it got, the thinner the shard became. The frosted yellowness of it thickened into a green-tinged tip.

As the last of it exited his third eye, so did a single drip of blood. His head spun, then the room...

**

The next thing he knew, he was on the floor of the bathroom. Déjà vu hit him as he kind of remembered being in this same position before. Maybe yesterday, maybe earlier today. He didn't know; he couldn't remember.

He looked down, wondering why he was so cold. His body was covered in the same thick sheen of grease as before. *Fuck, it wasn't just a hangover induced nightmare,* he thought as his eyes fell on the blood encrusted around his crotch. Panic hit him like a fast-moving bus when he couldn't see his dick in the blood, but he calmed when he saw the pathetic, frightened little thing cowering in his bloody, greasy pubic thatch.

He had toyed with the idea of shaving his pubes, he'd read somewhere that it made a man's manhood look larger for the ladies, but he didn't think he would ever live it down if Mick ever found out about it. He would get called baldy-cock or ten-year-old boy for the rest of his life.

However, none of that mattered, small and pathetic or not, it was still there, attached to him, and that was all right with him.

He remembered then why he'd fallen over.

He gazed at whatever it was in his hands that he had pulled from his old chap like a magician pulling multi-coloured handkerchiefs from his sleeves.

The thing was the length of one of his fingers and thinned out to a vicious looking bloody point. Not wanting to, but needing to, he reached down and pulled back his crusted foreskin. The slit in the head where he had excavated this thing from was dribbling. It was thick, and it was pink, like blood was mixing with the horrible gunk that he was covered in. As he pulled the skin right back, a thick glob of it, not quite transparent, dripped and landed on his thigh. He watched as it slipped down the greased-up rash-covered flesh of his inner thigh.

He stood up, maybe a little too fast as his head was still spinning, and hung his little Petey, as his mum used to call it, over the toilet. The ooze was still oozing and was ready to drip into the toilet water beneath him.

He watched as it fell with fascination, albeit a morbid one.

The bloody, fatty discharge hit the water and instantly solidified. It changed into a drip-shaped ball before bobbing back to the surface surrounded by a greasy film.

His bladder began to scream again.

He placed the discoloured shard on the top of the cistern, for some reason carefully, as if scared to break it. With two fingers, he urged his shrunken, shy, and misused cock out of its hiding place. He really needed to piss now, more than anything else in the world.

He swallowed hard, leaned one hand against the wall behind the toilet, and positioned himself to go. There was a tingle in the nub of his penis, but he cast that aside for now as the urge to piss was suddenly everything in his life.

He took a deep breath and let himself go.

Nothing happened.

Closing his eyes, he envisioned himself on a beach with the water lapping at the shore. It was a technique he used while at the football game and he had to piss in the urinals. Stage fright was what it was. It didn't always happen, but when it did, it was the worst thing in the world.

"Daddy, why is that man standing there? He's got his thingus out, but he's not having a wee-wee."

It happened to him once, when he was about eighteen, and he had never been able to forget it.

He slowed his breathing and concentrated. Anticipating a full stream of hot, yellow urine that smelt like a certain breakfast cereal, he was more than a little baffled when still nothing happened!

He was becoming desperate now. His bladder was poised and set to release its cargo, but nothing would flow. He flexed his stomach muscles, attempting to force it out, but all this did was send cramps through his body. He tickled at the crack of his ass— when he was a child, this would sometimes release the muscles in his urethra and release the flow. But still there was nothing. He was beginning to sweat. The stink of the grease covering him and mixing with his sweat was making him hungry and sick at the same time. It smelt like a bad takeaway meal left to go cold overnight.

His stomach was beginning to swell. He wanted to see, to witness this change, but was loathe to look at the white film covering him. He could feel the pee in his bladder sloshing around, seeming to want to flow just as much as he wanted it to. Tears filled his eyes. This was the worst he had ever needed to piss in the whole of his life.

He tickled the crack of his behind again, praying it would work.

And this time, it did. To his relief, his bladder opened, and he could feel the piss trickling towards the light at the end of its shrivelled tunnel. He tried to relax, but the woozy feeling in his head kept bringing him out of it. It was spinning and throbbing and making him unsteady.

When his bladder began to release, as his water came closer to exiting, an agony tore through his penis, the likes of which he had never experienced before. He yelled in pain, in blinding torture. His wide eyes flicked downwards in time to witness a dense yellowish sludge dribble from his tip. It looked like vegetable oil pouring from a bottle, and it stunk to high heaven. It was something he had never smelt before and hoped to never smell again.

The sludge continued to seep, bringing the fresh agony of its release with it.

The discharge was sluggish as it leached from his dick. His stomach muscles were flexing, again and again, involuntarily, as his body attempted to expel the pungent poison as fast as it could. Only the release was thicker than his urethra, and he felt like it was tearing his cock apart from the inside.

Eventually, the torment in his bladder, his cock, his stomach, and his head began to abate. As his head stopped spinning and his vision began to return to something resembling normality, he was revolted to see the sheen of grease covering his skin was bubbling with moisture as his body was covered in sweat. The stink of it mixing with the grease was simply horrible; he didn't have another word for it, it literally made him balk. This scared him as he knew there was nothing left for him to chuck up. He didn't think his stomach could take any more violence right now, *or ever,* he thought.

The sludge was still pushing out of his thin slit like the world's worse toothpaste being pushed out of a pinkish/white fleshy tube.

Eventually, the flow trickled to nothing. Through one eye, he looked into the toilet. The vile discharge had solidified in the fetid water. It was a wet, bloated slug, floating, slinking just below the surface. He willed his arm to reach out and flush the toilet. He was glad it was out of him, but he still needed it gone. As the surging water flushed away his ablution, he sighed, not enjoying the stinging throb of his poor penis.

As the water settled, it left a film of grease resting on the surface. The slug he'd expelled hadn't mixed well with the water, separating like water and oil.

He waited a few moments, just staring wide-eyed and blankly into the bowl, waiting for the cistern to fill so he could flush again.

When the water finally settled, the film was still there.

With a roar, he slammed the lid of the toilet down, instantly wishing he hadn't; his headache hit his eyes, and he felt them throbbing, bulging in their sockets. He turned his attentions to the shower. He reached out a milky-white, grease-bound arm and turned it on. His fingers slipped on the knob, but sheer persistence helped him to turn it, making the spray as hot as he thought his body could handle.

Stepping out of his greasy underwear, doing his best not to look at his coated groin and the blubber congealing in his pubic hair, he stepped carefully into the shower. It took him a moment to make sure his slick feet didn't slip on the white plastic of the bath. The steam coming from the water hit his nose, and he breathed deep. He wanted, no, he needed this shower more than anything. He just wanted to feel human again. With his hands resting against the tiles on the walls for support, no matter how precarious it was, he stepped into the cascading warmth. The water burned him where it touched, but after everything he had been through, it was mostly an enjoyable sensation. What he didn't enjoy was the smell coming from his flesh where the water caressed it.

It smelt like he was cooking. Like his skin had turned into old burgers, stinking like the dirtiest café where the owner hadn't ever changed the fat. It sickened him, his delicate stomach was performing somersaults, but it also made him hungry for the first time in two days.

Using one of Mary's body sponges, he scrubbed himself, his arms moving more freely in the hot water than they had all day. He scrubbed and scrubbed, and then scrubbed some more. He could imagine his flesh flaying from his bones, such was the intense heat and the power he was putting into the wash. The feel of the rash, even underneath the sponge, was sickening, made worse due to the outer layer of fat dripping down his body as the heat liquified it. The soap was useless at penetrating the stubborn underlying layer, so he scrubbed harder, fighting a losing battle. All he was doing was rubbing the lard deeper into his skin and redistributing it around his body.

It was not washing off.

Realising the futility of what he was doing, never mind the stinging of his scathed and scalded skin, he stepped out of the shower. Forgetting his feet were coated in the white stuff, he slipped.

Reaching out, he grabbed at the thin shower curtain to stop himself falling. It was a useless gesture as it was only fixed to the rail it hung from by thin plastic hooks, and as his fingers gripped the fabric, with his weight depending on it to support him, they all gave way. The shower curtain ripped from the rail, and he completed his fall back into the bath, knocking his head against the tiled wall.

Stars filled his vision, and he felt something give on his face.

It was an odd sensation, one that he couldn't relate to anything else, but it was the only way his addled brain could describe it.

Something *gave*!

CHAPTER
—7—

"**I** said I'm working from home, OK?" Mick shouted into the phone. He was on speakerphone as for some reason—one that he couldn't fathom and therefore angered him like nothing else—he couldn't grab the device and keep hold of it. His fingers were coated in something that he couldn't get off. In fact, his whole body was coated in it.

It stunk like the worst thing he had ever smelt in his life, and he had gone down on an unwashed dwarf in Amsterdam on a bet with his mates on his stag do. *The one that Finn wasn't* allowed *to go on,* he fumed in his head. That had stunk to high heaven. She was a delicacy over there. Not as famous as the old bird in Benidorm, in Spain, who shoved razor blades up herself, but The Stinky Stump was not far behind.

The bet was to lick her out for a full five minutes. The whole time his tongue had to be in contact with some part of her labia. Christ it was horrible. The legend was that she used to rub feta cheese and tinned sardines into herself beforehand, just to enhance the experience.

If you managed five minutes, the drinks were free for the rest of the night, for up to six people.

He'd done seven minutes and thirty-five seconds.

Apparently, it was a record.

That night, he had the numbers tattooed onto his shoulder. When Paula asked about them the night of the wedding, he feigned drunken amnesia. It had never been forgotten, and, apparently, it had never been beaten.

The following year, they went back for the stag anniversary, and he had another go. This time, the stump was clean, and he was down there for a good half an hour. She told him she'd cum four times, but he thought she was just telling him that. The state her fanny had been in, he didn't think she'd cum in years.

Still, it was a lasting memory!

"I'm not feeling good," he said, half smiling at the memory of *his* stump sliding into that little bundle of fun. Regardless of his headache and the relentless pains in his stomach, the stum had made him feel a little better. "Yeah, put my calls on hold, and I'll speak to everyone tomorrow. This bug will have passed by—" He didn't finish his sentence as a sharp pain tore through his abdomen. All he could do was retch.

He leaned forwards, opened his mouth, and his stomach did the rest.

"Mick..." the tinny voice from the phone said. "Mick, are you OK?"

He couldn't answer as he couldn't breathe. His stomach was pushing something up from its darkest depths. It was thick; it felt solid as his muscles worked extra hard to expel it.

"Mick, do you want me to call an..."

With an almighty heave that knocked him off the bed, something forced its way out of his mouth.

It was not like any vomit he had ever done before. It was not like any vomit he had ever even heard of before. He couldn't breathe. His pipes were completely blocked, throat and nose. He was panicking and could feel himself turning red, then pink as his body forced this *thing* out of him. He thought it was going to split his lips, it was that solid.

His body was working extra time to expel whatever it was, and he was just a passenger on that journey; there was nothing he could do but try to push, to pass this *object*.

His vision was darkening, black lights were exploding in his peripheral, yet still his body heaved.

Then, suddenly, it was over.

The thickness in his gullet narrowed, and whatever it was he had just birthed from his mouth slid out onto the bedroom floor. He lay, his face buried into the carpet, gasping for breath. His body felt like he had just gone fifteen rounds toe to toe with Muhammed Ali, who Mick considered to be the greatest fighter he had ever seen. His fingers, his toes, his chest, his hips, but most of all his throat, were all almost numb. Not the nice numb that came after a few lines of coke and some brandy, this was a nasty numb where he couldn't tell if he was even still alive.

He thought his vision was floating back to normality as he could see a great big lump of... he didn't know what it was. All he knew was that it had come out of him.

"Mick, come on, mate... speak to me."

The call was still connected. With strength that he really didn't have, he knocked the leg of the table the phone was on, and the device dropped from it. It landed in the thick chunk of whatever it was he had been carrying in his stomach.

The off-white jelly splattered as the phone landed in it, splashing his face and adding the God-awful stink of his life.

The impact in the jelly-vomit disconnected the phone, and he didn't have it in him to move his heavy arms to attempt to retrieve it.

As he lay there on the carpet with foul gunge still dribbling from his mouth and sinking into the fibres all around him, his eyes were on the ugly thing before him, the one with his mobile phone sticking out of it. He closed his throbbing eyes and exhaled through his nostrils. For the first time in his miserable life, Mick had to admit something to himself. He hated it, but it was time it was acknowledged.

He was scared.

.

CHAPTER
—8—

Finn watched the streaming water. It rushed towards him clear and ran away a different colour. It wasn't the pink he would have expected it to be, given how hard he had hit his head on the bath. It reminded him of when he washed the crack of his ass in the shower when he hadn't wiped himself thoroughly.

The water was beige.

Please, don't let me have shit myself again, he thought, closing his eyes before the tears he could feel welling had a chance to fall and add to the surging hot water all around him.

When he re-opened them, he saw something.

It was in the water. It was moving, slowly, with the force of the stream. It was brown and maybe three inches in length. At first, he thought he *had* shit himself again and the little brown thing was a turd that had escaped him in the fall, making its way, slowly but surely, towards him on its journey to the plug hole. He took in a deep breath, swallowing a mouthful of water at the same time.

Then he noticed the curvature of the little brown thing didn't look like any turd he'd ever had the misfortune of seeing before. No, this had a strange curve to it, and it was almost flat.

It took him a moment before he realised he was looking at an ear!

His ear.

Panic surged through him most when he realised it wasn't attached to his head.

It was in the bath, being pushed towards the plughole by the rush of warm water.

He didn't want to, but his hand betrayed him and reached up to his face. He felt around for his ear but only found a tear in his flesh where the appendage used to be. He pushed himself up, slipping in the process before getting himself into a sitting position. He reached to the window ledge at the far end of the bath and grabbed the shaving mirror. It was difficult to gain purchase of the silver stand as his hands felt like they were covered in shower-gel.

Naked, shivering even though it was hot, and not amused, he checked his face. It was still coated in the strange white coating. Beneath the white sheen, his face was covered in the odd rash that was covering his body, and there was a slurry of brown sludge cascading down one side of his face. Frantic, he clawed at the grease, trying to clear it away, wanting to see the wound. As he wiped at the fat, he cleared a small area, allowing him to see the gaping hole in his head. It was deep, and it was ragged; the ear had been roughly torn away, yet he felt no pain. He should be in agony right now, but he wasn't.

His breathing was shallow, the rising panic was lurking just below his surface, and he was amazed he could still think rationally. After a short struggle with his heavy arms, goading them into doing more work than they wanted to, he finally managed to get out of the bath without killing himself. He looked at the water that hadn't yet disappeared down the plughole and saw a thin film of grease covering it, very much like the water in the toilet.

He looked at his hands, and then his body.

Where he had scrubbed at the white, it was back. It covered his naked torso from top to bottom. He looked at his penis; the thick sludge oozing out of his slit was disgusting. It reminded him of a film he'd seen as a kid, where someone found a dead body with slugs slithering out of it.

"What the fuck *is that*?" he sobbed, his jaw hurting as his mouth moved.

Everything was hurting today.

His hand caressed his neck. He could feel it was swollen, and it was now difficult for him to swallow. He thought about the thick gunk dripping from his cock and wondered if the same shit was closing his throat. He leaned over the bath and heaved as he hawked deep from his chest and spat it into the stagnant water.

It was difficult to eject the spit from his mouth. Not only because his lips now seemed to be acting of their own accord, but the spit was too thick to pass between them.

As another panic began to rear its ugly head, he put his fingers inside his mouth. Instantly, his tastebuds bloomed, and saliva filled the cavity. He could feel the spit, it was thick, like a small piece of vomit that hadn't quite made it out. He knew that was impossible, his stomach had been emptied, completely, by his excessive vomiting. He reached, causing himself to gag again before catching it. His finger pushed in, squeezing it like a ball of putty or that horrible slime the kids loved so much. The sensation of pulling it from his mouth was alien to him, but it came easily. He rested it in the palm of his hand and looked at it.

It was a misshapen ball of fat.

That's what it was.

There was no denying that now.

It looked like he had dug his hands into the fat fryer and pulled out a semi-solid fat ball.

His throat was closing over. The walls of his oesophagus were constricting. Swallowing was now an effort. His breathing was becoming laboured. His hands went to his throat. It, too, was swollen. He could no longer feel his Adam's apple, just the roughness of his skin beneath the slick, cold covering of slime coating every inch of his body.

A horrible thought passed through his brain.

If the gunk was sliding out of his dick, what was happening around the back?

He reached around. His eyes closed, hoping beyond hope that he wasn't leaking the same fatty substance from back there.

He was!

It was wet, and it was pliable. He could feel it squeezing out of his hole like an ice cream dispenser dumping its load of fat-laced Mr Whippy into an ice cream cone. He tried to squeeze his ass closed, and although he had *some* control of it, all he managed to do was to thin the rivulet of grease dripping from him.

Have I got a virus? he thought; *No*, he hoped as he brought his hand around to look at was secreting from his anus. It was the same fat as from his mouth and penis, only it was beige and mixed with faeces.

A flu would explain the gunk coming up from my chest, although I don't remember any flu that would cause this to seep out of my cock and arse.

He was trying to convince himself, and although not relishing the prospect of a week or so in bed, wracked with aches and pains, it was a better alternative than what was happening to him now.

On slippery feet, he pulled himself up to a standing position. His aching bones physically cracked and then popped as the cartilage between them stretched.

He shuffled over to the mirror, intending to open his mouth to inspect his tonsils, to see if they, too, were swollen. Only when he looked into the glass, he got the fright of his life.

One side of his face was pouring with brown sludge from where his ear used to be, and the rest of it was coated with a pure stark white. He looked like the victim of a prank and some emulsion paint. He wiped at the grease, looked at his skin beneath. It was covered in the same rash that had attacked the rest of his body.

His ear, his stomach and legs, his throat! *What the fuck is happening here?* he asked himself, getting away from the horror in the mirror. He was hoping his eyes had been playing cruel tricks on him and that he didn't really look that bad. He hoped that rubbing them before looking again might cure him of the affliction he'd just witnessed, that it had just been his brain playing ticks on him in his weakened state. Punishment for drinking too much.

It wasn't!

As his reflection stared back at him, the raised, raw skin and the thick brown blood were all still there.

He wanted to crawl away from it all, he longed to climb back into bed, to hide beneath the covers, to slink back into the darkness of this nightmare so he could wake up again and everything would be normal. But by the time he made it back to the bedroom and saw the greasy covers still wet from whatever it was coating his flesh, he knew the nightmare he was in was a woke one.

There would be no sleeping through this one, no waking up thinking it was an awful dream and laughing about it with Mary. Nope, this was what he looked like now, coated in a sheen of who-knows-what with a nasty rash over his entire body, discharge seeping from the front and the back... and only one ear.

A shudder ran through him.

His body sagged; every bone ached. His ear was gone, although he wasn't really feeling any pain, his lower regions were oozing gunk, and he stunk to high Heaven.

"What have I done to deserve this?" his mumbled through his greasy tongue and swollen throat as his wet fingers caressed the area where once there had been an ear.

His heart was thudding in his chest. It was only a slow thudding, but it took breath from him with each beat, like he had been running or some other kind of strenuous activity. He could feel himself getting smaller and smaller with the pulsating rhythm. He attempted to take a deep breath, but it caught in his chest, and another moment of panic gripped him as he lost all the air in his body.

He coughed.

As he did, something inside him dislodged.

He didn't know if that was the correct term for what had happened, but it seemed right to him.

He coughed again, and whatever it was flew from his mouth and splattered onto the vomit- and shit-stained carpet next to the bed.

Through misty eyes, he looked at it.

The carpet had been beige the day before his night out with Mick; it had been a pristine, spotless beige. Now it was many colours, most of them dull, grimed and ground into the fabrics, but this colour was something new. It stood out within the different shades of brown.

It was both dark and bright-red at the same time.

As he looked at it, his hand involuntarily ventured to the side of his face, where his fingers once again rimmed the painless, torn, exposed flesh of the remains of his ear.

He'd never seen an internal organ before, not in real life. He'd watched programmes on TV, operations, murders, and the like; but never had he seen something so... vivid!

Not to mention disgusting.

It was raw meat, sitting in a setting where raw meat had no business being. It was like seeing a palm tree in the tundra. But what made this worse was the fact it had come from *him!* It was a part of his insides.

He had no idea what organ it was, or if it was a vital one. In truth, he didn't know if it was an organ at all; it was just a clump of meat, splattered in a red wetness, soaking into the carpet.

Mary is going to fucking kill me, was all he could think.

The bizarreness of this being his only thought when his vital organs were expelling from his mouth was not lost on him. He bent closer, taking a better look at what it was lying accusingly on his carpet.

His bones creaked as he bent his back. This was nothing new to him. He was in his forties now and had come to terms with the ugly noises his body made, but these cracks were different. For starters, they came accompanied with sharp, agonising pain. He stood up, his hands rushing to the small of his back as he shouted in agony.

The pain didn't recede like he was expecting.

Instead, it lingered, it throbbed, and it grew. Before he knew it, he was doubled over. Flashbacks of the day before as the hangover tore through his body, ravishing his stomach and ripping it to shreds, flashed through his consciousness. This was worse than yesterday. It was sharp, cutting, like something tearing at his insides, trying to escape its confines, or as if he'd swallowed glass and it was happily slicing his innards into ribbons.

He fell.

The agony of his kneecaps smashing to the floor was lost within the torture of what was happening internally. He opened his mouth to scream, but he couldn't. There was something stuck in his throat. He tried to scream again, but whatever it was blocked all sounds. His stomach heaved, another involuntary push, and it worked. It dislodged whatever it was, and it shot out of his mouth.

It landed with a splat next to whatever the other thing was on the carpet. Now there were two lumps of clotting flesh, accusing him of God only knew what. He couldn't take his eyes off them as he wiped his drooling chin. He wasn't surprised to see his grease covered hand covered in blood. Within the course of an hour, he had become enveloped in a greasy coating, a horrible rash, there was some crazy vileness secreting from his cock and arsehole, he'd lost an ear, and now he was throwing up internal organs onto the carpet.

It was enough for him to consider giving up.

After his expulsion, the pains in his stomach ebbed, but a sound like a washing machine emptying issued from his stomach, and he felt something shifting inside. He braved a look down; the sludge was still seeping from his cock, and he could feel the discharge around the back intensifying.

It was a strange feeling. Once the agony deteriorated, the feeling wasn't too unpleasant.

With a shaky breath, he looked around the room. He knew his mobile phone was somewhere near, he never, ever let it out of his reach. He tried to think of the last time he'd had it. All he could remember was when they were in the pub and Mick was threatening the old couple.

Jesus, that feels like a hundred years ago.

The device was on the floor, where he'd dropped it after vomiting all over it while on the videocall with his boss.

It might as well have been a million miles away.

He would have to pass the two lumps of... whatever it was he'd thrown up... to get to it. A journey of just few yards, but not one he relished.

He looked at his white-coated feet. His legs resembled off-white candles that had been used. Drips of the filth were issuing from his crotch and penis. He breathed deep from his nose; his stink was either passing or he had become nose-blind to it. He guessed the latter. Willing his feet to work, he took a baby step towards where his phone was, towards potential help for whatever he was going through.

He diverted his eyes from the bloody clumps, avoiding them as if they were dangerous animals that could attack him at any time—for all intents and purposes, to him, they could be dangerous as he didn't have any idea *what* they were. He made his way slowly to the side of the bed, his toes squelching from the wetness covering them and the dampness of the carpet.

His reactions were sorely tested as the vomit-spattered phone slipped from his oleaginous grip and it hit the floor again. He was far too slow, and the effort hit him hard. As he watched the black glass brick bounce undamaged on the carpet, he found himself dizzy and out of breath.

After a moment, he bent down to retrieve it, and his back cracked again.

Another agony in his stomach came with it, as did the feeling of something shifting in his stomach again.

Hoping to just curl up and die, he readied himself for the hideous feelings in his stomach to return; he was shocked and harrowed as whatever it was didn't come up through his throat.

It went the other way.

The sudden cramps that hit him were worse than before. They were hot, stabbing pains. His insides were in turmoil; liquid fire was bubbling and burning, melting the linings of his stomach and bowel.

He needed to go to the toilet rather badly, but he was too scared. *If it feels this bad inside, what will it feel like coming out?*

He fell face first onto the carpet, and his mobile phone hit his temple. He screamed as his body twisted into a foetal position, his arms trying to find purchase on his slippery legs to hold them close. The movement he'd felt in his stomach was back.

A gurgle ensued, and something slid from his inside to the outside.

Burning, red hot pokers from Hell pierced him as something slipped, almost effortlessly, from his anus. It was wet, slimy, and painful. Tears were blurring his vision, but he didn't need to look to know what had happened. He'd never heard of it before, he couldn't remember talking about something like this in *any* conversation he'd ever had with anyone. However, two words flashed through his head. They fit this situation perfectly.

Those words were... prolapsed rectum!

In his mind's eye, he saw a rosy-red apple protruding from his arsehole. He didn't know where the image came from, maybe it was something he'd seen on the internet, he didn't know. But he could imagine his wrinkled sphincter stretching, tearing, as blood, dark and fresh, dripped from the hole.

The sobs came suddenly, but they soon took over his entire body.

"What's happening to me?" he whispered in between bubbles of thick, almost chewy saliva forming in the corners of his mouth. They combined with the stream of fatty mucus streaming from his nose. "Why me?" he asked. "Why me?"

The pain in his stomach ebbed. He needed help and he needed it right now. His phone was next to his head. He could see it; the black screen was covered in grease, but he knew it would be fully charged. He didn't want to unwrap his arms from his legs. He had a feeling he might fall apart if he did, but simply shouting *help* from where he was lying wouldn't do.

The sucking noise as he removed his arm from his leg was disgusting, but he continued to reach out a shaky hand, hoping to control it enough to make a call to his wife.

His glazed hand gripped the thin glass brick. He wiped the stomach juices that were covering the screen, and it lit up. He looked at the picture on the screen; it was him, Mary, and the kids at the beach, each with an ice cream in their hands. There were seagulls circling in the background, and he remembered the day perfectly. One of the gulls had swooped down and grabbed Rob's ice cream. Even though he screamed at the time, they'd all laughed about it later.

Later that night, he and Mary had made love in their small room while their children slept, snoring, in the next room.

It had been a fantastic holiday.

That was before his greasy skin, before the rash, before he'd lost an ear in the shower, and before his rectum had prolapsed while he lay on the floor of his bedroom.

Lying on his side, his rectum hurt too much to lie on his back, he made the phone call.

"What?" Mary asked on the other end. It was just one word, but Finn heard everything in it that he needed to.

"Marwy..." he breathed into the phone. It was then he realised he couldn't talk correctly. He sounded like John Merrick in that fucked up black and white film from years ago. His tongue felt twice the size it was supposed to be. No, forget that, it was at least four times bigger. He ran it over the roof of his mouth, detesting the feeling that was akin to eating cold slices of lamb on a Sunday evening after the roast. The meat would still taste lovely, but the fat from it would coat the roof of his mouth.

"Finn, is that you messing about? If it is, It's not funny."

"Marwy..." he breathed again.

"Look, I'm in work, so stop arsing about. What do you want? It had better be good, or a maybe even a fucking apology..."

"Marwy... I'm thick!"

"Look, if this is one of Finn's mates playing a game, *Mick*..." the last word was spat; even in his desperate state he could hear her disdain for Mick. "...then It's fucking hilarious, but I don't have time for games, goodbye!"

The line went dead.

"What? Marwy!" he tried to shout down the phone.

He knew why she'd reacted like she had. His voice was different, and he was having problems forming words correctly. He dropped the arm holding the phone, and another level of agony gripped him.

He tried to straighten his back and neck, but his movements were severely limited.

"Jesuth," he sputtered.

It wasn't his voice. There was a wetness to it. Like his chest was filled with phlegm and it was drowning his voice before he could breathe life into it. He coughed, attempting to rid himself of the frog, or the toad, that was residing down there. As he did, something else dislodged inside him. He closed his eyes, scoffed miserably. There was a click and a searing pain. He had never been stabbed before, but he was willing to bet his whole mortgage that it felt like this. He coughed again, involuntarily, and whatever had dislodged in his chest moved. He couldn't breathe now; whatever it was had lodged in his throat.

His loss of breath was just another milestone in his *fucking* fantastic day, and he honestly deliberated just lying there on the filthy carpet and allowing himself to suffocate. It would be over in a few minutes, all this pain, all the vileness happening to him would be done. Yes, it would be awful for Mary to find him with one ear and the contents of his stomach hanging out of his asshole, and yes, it would be harrowing for the boys, but right now, he didn't give a shiny fuck about any of them. All he wanted was for this pain to be over.

He began to convulse. His chest heaved as his body gasped for life-giving air. He could feel his eyes bugging in their sockets. He wanted to close them, to shut out the whole world, but couldn't.

There was a flash of light. He didn't know where it came from, but his vision in one eye had become milky at best. A million shards of molten metal stabbed his brain as warmth flooded down his face. Even in his raptures of torture, he had an idea what had happened.

One of his eyes had popped.

Is this it? He hoped it was.

His mouth flooded with thick, cold wetness, and he was forced into an involuntary vomit. He needed to sit up; his head was spinning from the lack of air.

He'd forgotten about his prolapsed rectum, and the apple hanging from his arse dragged across the carpet.

Pain lit up his one-eyed vision, and as he opened his mouth to scream, something flew out.

As it flew, he involuntarily gasped in huge lungful's of sweet oxygen. He choked again as, in his body's desperation to survive, he aspirated some of the bitter bile that was filling his mouth. Once the coughing fit was over, he looked at what he had brought up this time.

He was expecting another clump of bloody organ that his body had deemed unnecessary.

But it wasn't.

It *was* a thick clump, but this one was different. It was fatty.

He tore his eye away from it, he had to; otherwise, he felt he would slip into insanity with a one-way ticket. It sounded like a fucking great idea.

He reached out and pushed the door to the wardrobe that ran the length of the bedroom wall. It took him every last bit of strength to do it as, much like his tongue, his arms and legs were also feeling too big for his body. They simply refused to work as they should.

The door swung open, and he managed to see himself in the mirror on the back of it.

He regretted it.

Through the mist and the blood coursing from his ruined, popped eye, the monster that was staring back at him petrified him.

His face was barely recognisable. His head was filthy, covered in goo and blood from his ear, and now also from his eye. His face was swollen and was no longer symmetrical with only one eye. His skin was coated in the white fat, and his ruined eyehole drooped. Brown stuff—he thought of it as shit—was pouring from the socket.

He was every boogieman he had ever feared in his life. He was Freddie Kruger, a burnt Jason Voorhies; he was Seth Brundle from *The Fly*... all of them mixed into one hideous, living, breathing abomination.

The worst part of it all was that it was him!

There was no denying it. He wasn't a special effect. He wasn't an actor in the best makeup he had ever seen in his life. It was *him*, and he was living this nightmare.

I need a doctor! he thought, looking at the grease-bound mobile phone lying in the puddle of bloody spit, regurgitated fat, and the brown secretions of what was dripping from his ear and eye.

With a Herculean effort, not the least of it due to the slickness of his hands, he grabbed the device and attempted to unlock it again. His thumb print wouldn't work. His eye recognition wouldn't either. He had to type the numbers for the four-digit code, and he had to do it three times as his fingers slid each time, entering the wrong number.

Eventually, he unlocked it and managed to find the number for the doctor in his contacts.

He pressed the call button.

After seven attempts, all of them engaged, a perky female voice surprised him. "Good morning, surgery," the voice on the other end said.

Morning? He thought. *It's the end of the fucking world.* "Hullo..." he croaked. "Do you have any appointmenths available for today, pleath?"

"I'm sorry, sir, but I didn't quite catch that. Can you repeat the question?"

"I thaid, do you have any appointmenths available for thith morning, pleath!"

"I still didn't get that. I'm so sorry!"

"Appointmenths... how fucking hard ith that? It'th your thucking job! Are there any appointmenths availa—Oh thuck it," he shouted, terminating the call. In his anger to disconnect, his phone slid from his hands.

As he leaned over to pick it up, his head began to swim again, his stomach flipped, his exposed rectum itched and throbbed. His eye continued to bleed, and his lost ear ached and itched.

He fell onto the carpet again, bashing his nose against the floor. More stars flashed before his eyes, and his stomach began to dance again—the dance he knew would end up with him on his hands and knees with something forcing its way out of his mouth.

He reached a feeble hand out for his phone, needing the comfort he could get from it, but the torrent of agony from his entire body caused him to pass out before he could reach it.

CHAPTER
—9—

Her first thought was *Has Finn been cooking?*

This made her smile. That he hadn't been well and had dragged himself out of bed and actually made dinner, just so she didn't have to, it was a nice thing for him to do.

As she hung her coat in the little cupboard, she noticed the house wasn't as warm as it might be if someone had been cooking. *Take-away then?* she thought as she removed her outdoor shoes, eagerly anticipating her slippers.

"Finn, are you in?" she shouted, noting there were no kids running to greet her at the door, which was the norm. Another nice thought crossed her romantic mind. Maybe he'd left them at her mum's, where they went after school. *A take-away, no kids... I know where this is leading. Dirty bastard,* she thought with a salacious grin. It had been a while since they'd spent any quality time together.

She popped her head into the living room. The smile on her face was so wide it was in danger of splitting her head in two. She was expecting something goofy happening in there, like Finn, wearing nothing but a tie, sat at the dining table with a large slap-up meal set out before him.

The room was empty; however, she could still smell the food. She looked up the stairs and shouted him again. "Finn, are you up there?"

She noted then that the smell wasn't quite as delicious as she'd first assumed. Now it smelt old. Like how a cold burger and fries from Finn's favourite outlet smelt if it had been left for an hour or so.

It was beginning to offend her nose, like it was crawling up her nostrils and leaving a residue up there, coating them somehow. It was beginning to turn her stomach.

"Jesus Christ!" she shouted, more in disappointment than anger. The small pang of excitement—and could she say *horniness? Yes... why not horniness*—was gone, leaving only a black hole where there once was hope. "What have you been doing in here? Have you been eating upstairs? Have you even been to work?"

There was no answer.

"Finn, are you even in?" she shouted, holding her nose, as the smell seemed to be becoming physical.

She stepped on the first stair, huffed at the silence she received as a reply, and began her accent. The stink got heavier the further up she went. It was so bad near the top that merely holding her nose was no longer cutting it. Whatever the smell was, she could taste it and feel the greasiness in her mouth.

"Finn? I swear... if you're stinking up that bedroom, I'll..." She didn't finish her threat as she saw the wet marks on the carpet between the bedroom and the bathroom. "Fucking hell?" she hissed. "Can't you take a towel into the bathroom with you?" she continued, still holding her nose.

She tutted as she entered the bathroom and saw the mess in there. The wetness from the carpet continued onto the tiled floor, only there, it changed. It turned thick and off white, like he'd squeezed her body cream all over the floor. It was white, but there was a hint of yellow and beige within it. She took her hand away from her nose, forgetting about the funk in the air as she wanted to clean up this mess.

She gagged. The stink was so profuse, she could feel it coating her nostrils and her throat. She looked at the toilet. He had squirted her cream in there too.

It really was an ugly sight. She wondered what he could have been doing with it. *I bet its some weird sex shit,* she thought, thinking about how he had always been trying to get her to try new things. *But if it is, what the hell is that stink?*

"Finn, will you answer me, please?" she shouted again, her voice stern.

This time, she got her reply.

Or a semblance of one.

A low moan came from somewhere behind her.

Her skin covered in goosebumps as she turned to see where it was coming from. It reminded her of the strange phone call she'd received from him this afternoon. She didn't know what to expect, maybe something like the Creature from the Black Lagoon! She'd watched that film when she was a child; the half man, half fish monster had freaked her out so much that when the more recent film came out where the woman started having sexual relations with a similar monster, she couldn't believe people thought it had been romantic. She was even more perplexed when it had won awards. This stream of thought caught her by surprise, and she marvelled that her brain had gone there when she was so scared.

"Finn?"

Again, the response she received was a low, scary moan.

The goosebumps were back, this time stronger. Her skin felt tight, taught.

Tentatively, she took a single step towards the bedroom, following the grease stains in the carpet.

The floorboards under the carpet creaked.

She stopped.

The sound was too loud for her. For some reason she couldn't conceive, she didn't want whoever, or whatever, had made those horrible moans to know she was coming. She didn't want the Creature from the Black Bedroom springing out and either killing her or making mad, violent love to her.

She swallowed, tasting the nasty air, before taking another step. Her nose was adjusting to the oppressive aroma, but she didn't think she could get used to how *warm* the stench had become. Like the warm smell of chlorine when you enter a swimming pool... only this wasn't a clean smell, it was a dirty stink.

She took another step; there was another creak.

There was another moan, and her skin was instantly covered in cold sweat.

"Finn, stop messing about, will you? You're scaring me," she whispered, not completely sure it was him in the darkened room ahead of her. She knew *sometimes* his personal hygiene could be questionable, he tended to smell a little ripe occasionally, but the filthy atmosphere in there was a whole new low, even for him.

She took in a few rapid breaths and boldly stepped forward and turned the light on.

The scream sent her reeling backwards, back out onto the landing.

She didn't know if it came from her or from someone else. All she knew was she had walked into a warm, physical stench.

Then the scream came again.

This one was definitely *not* from her. She only knew this because her hand was over her mouth, stifling the shock, the horror, the utter revulsion, not to mention the moist air from entering her mouth more than it already had.

It was the thing on the floor in the bedroom that had been moaning.

It was on the floor, lying on its face. She thought it might have been human, but she couldn't be sure.

It was naked and pink. In the quick look she had gotten before staggering back, she had seen it was covered in a white lining, and there were... *things,* that was the only word she could use to describe what they were, seeping out of its—*Or is it his*—anus.

It resembled the worst tin of Spam she had ever seen in her life.

Whatever it was, it had turned its head, or what she thought of as its head, and looked at her. A hole had opened at the bottom of its face, and it... *It fucking mewled at me.* The sound was pathetic and heart-breaking at the same time.

"Finn?" she gasped, her voice hushed, breathless from the horror of what she was witnessing. The thing's body was long, cylindrical. She could see arms and legs, but they looked... *fused* was the only word that came to mind... with the rest of its body.

It was bending its torso, trying to flip itself over to look at her.

She would have run, probably should have, but there was something about the thing, something familiar.

It was her husband.

A small nub of what looked like a penis surrounded by slicked back pubic hair was pointing rigidly out from what she thought of as its front. A sickly sludge was seeping from it. She might have laughed, as it looked like a slow motion cum-shot from a porn film they had watched one time when they were trying to spice up their marriage—they'd had more fun rewinding and rewatching the money shot in slow-motion, screaming in hysterics as the spunk flew slowly off the girl's face and back into the guy's cock.

But this was not funny.

She had to remind herself that this was not a horror film.

Finn?

It was him. She knew it was him, the same way she could always tell her car in a crowded parking lot even though it was almost identical to every other car.

"Finn?"

This time, she spoke his name aloud.

It moved its *head* again, as if to answer.

Forgetting about the horrendous stink, she rushed forward towards what was left of her husband. It was too early for tears; she still hadn't gotten over the shock and the horror. All she could do was thank whoever needed thanking that the kids were not here to see this.

Suddenly, when she was almost to the thing, she stopped. A petrifying apprehension filled her, a sickly anxiety she could feel rising from hollow bones in her legs. It grasped at her stomach and, ultimately, her head.

She was scared. The closer she got to this thing, the more she was convinced it was her husband. Only, it wasn't *her* Finn, not anymore. His bloated body was pink, almost comically so, like a cartoon pig from one of their boy's silly children's programmes. But the pink was offset by the odd white film coating it.

The stench was coming from it. *From him,* she scolded herself as she stared at the undulating, contorting entity before her. Its mere presence was leaving a film of grease lining her mouth each time she breathed. It continued to twitch, and the sounds coming from the hole she surmised must have been his mouth were vile, horrible. It reminded her of the sound mutant rats might make—if she ever got to see any.

Her heart was pounding, and her goose-bump-covered skin was freezing cold.

She was stuck, rooted to the spot. She couldn't move even if she'd wanted to. Paralyzed in fear. She chuffed in her head at the things that were coming to her now.

"Mary," the thing that might have been Finn groaned.

It wasn't his voice. It was too deep and wet, like it was coming from an old man who had smoked ninety cigarettes a day for eighty years. Like a build-up of phlegm in his mouth that he couldn't release.

"Mary... help!" he groaned.

This time she recognised it. "Finn," she whispered and continued towards him slowly.

The closer she got, the worse the stink was. The secretions from its little nub of a penis intensified, and for the first time, she saw something red and bulbous protruding from its behind. This, too, was secreting white blubber. The stench was almost overpowering, and it stung her eyes, yet she knew she had to get to her husband. "What have you done? Are you...?"

She was going to finish with the question "OK?" but as her husband rolled over, her words got lost in her throat.

His face, beneath the layer of white, was swollen. His tongue, lolling out between two oversized lips, was fat. It looked like a shaved rat. He moved his head to look at her, and she saw a handful of white things fall from his mouth. At first, she thought it was more secretions from his mouth, but as they hit the carpet, she saw they were teeth. As she focused on them, she became aware of something else on the floor. Many *something elses*, actually. Her eyes roamed around the carpet, seeing the various clumps. There were a number of them. Big, heavy clumps of... what? Was it meat? It looked like raw steak. They were sitting on the carpet, redness dripping from them, seeping into the shag. Some were pink and wet, others purple and looked like they were drying. There were even a few that where white; these looked like masses of the same stuff that was covering Finn's body.

She covered her mouth, attempting to stifle the scream building inside her.

"Help... me," he croaked.

She reached out to him. She didn't want to touch him just in case whatever it was that was doing this to him was contagious.

He—*Or is he now an it?*—tried to move his arm, reaching out to touch her offered hand, but he couldn't. There was a sticky film of... she didn't know if it was skin or if it was the fatty substance that was all over him, connecting the limb to the main torso. The ugly, moist noise as his arm attempted to peel away from the rest of his body was a sound that she would take with her to the grave.

She wanted to push the fallen teeth back into his bleeding, fat-covered gums. She wanted to scrape away the filth and grime covering the man she loved. She wanted to make him normal again.

But she knew she couldn't.

This was still Finn, her husband, and she couldn't help herself. She wanted to give him something, even if it was just a connection with another human being. However, the thought of touching his naked body—something she had done many, many times over the years, touching him, caressing him, kissing him—made her want to vomit.

Her hands hovered over his body, and she toyed with the idea of running downstairs into the kitchen and slipping on the yellow gloves she used for washing the dishes; the thought of what his flesh was going to feel like brought a rush of saliva into her mouth, and to her shame, she retched.

This wasn't a subtle retch. It was a full, loud, physical retch that you would see on numerous sitcoms where something sickly but hilarious would happen to one of the protagonists. The fake audience would love it when they made the sound, and hilarity would ensue.

Not for her, though.

Eventually, she braved it and touched him. Her fingers tentatively touched his clammy skin and almost slid off him. He was wet, warm, and slippery. She knew if she wanted to hold him or turn him onto his back, she would have trouble gripping him.

But she knew she had to try. For one, the red, rosy apple protruding out of what she assumed was his anus was probably the worst thing she had ever seen in real life. Ever. The way the white filth was bubbling from all around it and from the little hole in the centre of it, she didn't think she would ever be able to look at a picture of a suckling pig again until the day she died.

Using her whole-body strength, not to mention considerable mental strength, she managed to turn him.

Once he was on his back, she wished she hadn't.

Her hands were slick, and the places her clothes contacted his naked flesh were wet with grease. His one remaining eye looked up at her. There was a sadness in that look, a desperation, fear of not knowing or understanding what was happening to him. As his swollen lips moved, maybe in an attempt to communicate with her, his tongue slipped out of the stinking hole.

It just kept slipping.

Bloated and brown, it slithered from his mouth like a sausage slipping from a sausage making machine. It just kept coming.

Eventually, it stopped and fell from his mouth in a curling strip. She looked at it.

It resembled a long slice of kebab meat. She knew it. She'd eaten enough of them over the years, with Finn, on their way home from the pub, in happier times, in times when her husband was still... what?

Human, was her only thought.

The sight of it, as his eye rolled in its socket to look at her, shocked her so much she leaned back onto the carpet in an attempted to put distance between her and the thing that had just fallen out of him. Her hands immersed into a puddle of crusting grease. As the tepid texture seeped between her fingers, she gagged again. She lifted it.

Yellowing puss dripped from between her fingers, leaving a snail-trail behind it. The trail was oily. This, along with the stink and the abomination of her naked, bloated, greased-up pig of a husband lying on the floor, scared her more than she'd ever been scared in her life.

She scrambled to her feet, no longer caring about the things residing on the carpet. She turned her back on the mewling aberration before her and ran into the bathroom. Vomit was burning her stomach, and her mouth was already filled with water. She fell to her knees, into the shit that was pooled around the toilet bowl, and looked in. There was a swirling, multi-coloured film residing on the surface of the water.

"Ma wee..." the groan from the bedroom beckoned her.

She shuddered, trying to stifle her impending hurl.

"Hep me..."

It didn't sound like Finn, but it did at the same time, and that never made any sense to her. Her head swimming with the thoughts of her new reality, she leaned over the toilet, hands on either side of it, and breathed deeply. Strangely enough, this was the least reeking place in the entire house. It wasn't easy to breathe, though, as each time she took in a breath, she could taste the vileness permeating through the air, coating the roof of her mouth.

How have I got here? she asked herself, her nose inches away from the filmy, stagnant toilet water. *Five minutes ago, I was smelling something lovely being cooked. Now, I am breathing in the stink from a toilet and my husband is a fucking living sausage.*

"Come on, Mary... come on!" she tried to coach herself. "That's Finn in there. Your husband. The father of your children. He needs your help. You can do this!"

Easing herself up from the toilet, amazed that she'd managed to keep what she had eaten for lunch down–*what did I have for lunch?* She couldn't remember that far back, it was years ago now, inconsequential–she left the bathroom. Not wanting to absorb the smell of the house, in case whatever it was he had *was* catching, she made her way to the stairs with the wet sleeve of her cardigan over her nose and mouth.

Too fucking late to cover your mouth now, she thought with a mental scoff.

Trying to ignore the pleading and whining of the plump, pink body that was occupying the bedroom as whatever Finn had become turned its head, attempted to reach out to her with its paddle-like arms, was difficult, but she had to get away from *it* for a moment. She ran into the kitchen and opened the cupboard door. She fished around inside for the facemasks she had inside, leftovers from the pandemic they had all just lived through, and slipped one onto her face.

"Closing the barn door after the horse has bolted," she mumbled under the light-blue material covering her face. Hurriedly, she fished in the pocket of the coat she'd taken off— something like ten years ago—by the front door and found her mobile phone. She opened the front door, stepped outside, and closed it quietly behind her.

A mild panic was building inside her, and she marvelled at how calm she was. *It will hit later,* she warned herself as she called an ambulance. Finn needed one, that much was obvious, but something inside her didn't want her to. She didn't want to know what was wrong with him. She wanted to just call a man with a van and for them to take him away and throw him into a river somewhere and be done with it. She would tell the kids that he had run off with another woman. They were young enough to forget about him. They could sell the house, start again somewhere new. She was relatively young enough. She could find another man, one that would treat her like the fucking princess she was, God-damn it. A man whose arms were not fused to his body by a film of fat that covered his whole body. A man without an apple sticking out of his arse; a man with two eyes *and a fucking tongue! Is that too much to ask?*

She stared at her phone, looking up only once to see an old couple who lived further up the street amble slowly past, a small dog pulling on an extendible leash running before them. The old woman looked at her, a half-smile forming on her face.

Mary could feel her tears welling.

That should be us when we reach that age.

Wiping the tears away, she looked down at her phone. Instead of dialling 9-9-9 for an ambulance or the police, she pressed an icon of a human head, and her contacts flashed up. She selected PAULA and put the phone to her ear.

As she did, the stink that came off her hands made her gag.

The phone rang a couple of times before it was answered.

"Mary... Oh, Mary, thank fuck you've rang," the manic female voice on the other end shouted. "Mary, It's Mick. He's really bad. I think he's—"

"Dying?" Mary finished for her.

Paula went quiet. An awkward silence hung between them. It was a moment or two before she spoke. "No, he's not dying, Mare! He's... he's, oh fuck, I don't know what he is. He stinks, really bad. I've called an ambulance. He's covered in—"

"Grease?" Mary interrupted again.

Once again, Paula went silent.

"I think they're dying," Mary said without a drop of emotion in her voice. "I'm lost, Paula," she admitted. "What can we do?"

"Have you called an ambulance? The hospital?" Paula pleaded. Mary had to move the device from her ear to stop herself from going deaf.

"Not yet," she replied. The calm she felt was strange. She was at peace with the world. She had just experienced the worst ten minutes of her life, but now, stood on the step of the house, free of the heavy atmosphere and the cloying stink, not to mention the human Cumberland sausage in the bedroom, she felt free.

"Dial nine-nine-nine right away!"

The screech from the device in her hands pulled her from her serene interlude, back into the stinking shithole that was her life.

"Tell them It's a fucking emergency. Mare, what the hell did these two drink on Sunday night?"

Mary pressed the red button on her phone, cutting off her banshee friend. She eyed the front door, then looked back at her phone.

A thought, it was only there for a moment, half a moment, maybe even less than that, but it was there. She could just drop her phone, stomp on it, smash everything that tied her to this life, including her boys, and just run. Run away, far away. Get to the airport. Fly far from everything, from Finn, from that foul stench, from the grease...

It was a fantasy; she knew it was impossible, but it *was* a nice thought.

Finn had his flaws, being easily led by Mick being one of the biggest, but she loved him regardless. *Maybe even because of those flaws,* she thought.

There was no way she could leave him like this.

She couldn't leave her boys, make them orphans, taken in by her parents while she lived a hedonistic, care-free lifestyle in a warmer clime.

With a sigh, she dialled 9-9-9 and asked for the ambulance service. She gave them some sort of explanation as to what was happening, explaining that they might need an infection team or something as it wasn't pretty in there. Then she put her phone away. She looked up at the sky, at the white trails the aeroplanes were making as they made their escapes. For the first time in a long time, she wished she smoked.

***

An ambulance was dispatched immediately.

CHAPTER
—10—

She watched as a paramedic ran, top speed, out of the house. He was a big man, dark skinned, who, before he went inside, had the look of someone who had seen it all. She'd tried to warn them but had been politely pushed to one side and asked nicely to stay out of their way.

Now, with projectile vomit splattering her neat little front path, the man's once dark skin now looked drained, ashen, almost grey. His eyes were of someone who had witnessed true madness, real terror.

The second paramedic, a slightly overweight woman, followed not far behind the first. Her blue gloves were clawing at her lighter blue facemask, similar to the one Mary had currently covering her chin. Her eyes met Mary's as she ran past, heading towards their vehicle.

The man, now recovered from his retching, joined his colleague at the ambulance. They were talking, chattering in excited tones, but she couldn't hear what they were saying.

Without even a look at her, they both disappeared into the back of the large yellow vehicle. Mary took a step closer to try to see what was happening, and they both emerged a few moments later with gowns over their green jump suits, masks in hand, and thicker, more industrial looking latex gloves. They smiled at her as they passed by, heading back into the house.

Their smiles never quite reached their eyes.

She followed them inside as they donned their masks and gloves. The smell hit her hard again—she had been outside for a while now and her immunity had waned. She gagged as the moist air forced itself into her.

Following them into the bedroom, she saw their eyes meet. It was just a fleeting moment, but it told Mary everything she needed to know. Her husband was a lost cause. She looked past them and at Finn, or what was left of him, lying naked, bloated, and pink, covered in an ugly rash, on her bedroom floor. She was mortified by his tiny penis head protruding from the top of legs, which looked like they were stuck together. Whatever it was covering his body was still oozing from its tip.

I used to love that cock! She shocked herself with this thought, but continued, regardless. *There was nowhere I didn't want it. In my mouth, between my legs, even a few times in places it was never supposed to go.*

The thought of sucking it now turned her stomach. Her mouth watered heavily, and she needed to spit. With her eyes closed, she swallowed the warm bitterness. As she did, she thought of the thick warmth of his cum in her mouth, how she would swallow it; but in her thoughts, it was no longer his semen, it was the stinking fat dripping from him now.

That was the last straw. She had been able to put it off until now, but this time, she had passed the point of no return.

She threw herself into the bathroom, ignoring the filth over the floor.

With her head plunged deep within the porcelain, she hurled until she was dry.

Then she cried.

She had wondered where her tears had been, when they would show themselves. She never thought they would be triggered by thoughts of giving Finn a blow job.

She felt a hand on her back, and she jerked.

It was the female paramedic. All she could see were her eyes over her mask, but she could see the sympathy in them. They were kind, but also wary. "Come on, love," she mumbled. "He's on the gurney. You're welcome to come with us in the rig, but we don't really know what we're dealing with here. It might be better if you followed in your car. Do you have anyone who can drive you?"

"No, I'll... erm, I'll be OK," she said with a nod.

"OK then, were going to take him to the Royal. Do you know the way? We're going to have our lights flashing and we'll be driving fast. We will lose each other."

She was nodding, her features like a rabbit in headlights. "Yeah, I know it."

"Good." She nodded. Mary could see the smile in her eyes. "We're going to take him down now and load him up. Go to Emergency Room One. It's an isolation unit, and he'll be there. You got that?"

Mary nodded again. "Room One," she repeated.

The two paramedics returned to the bedroom. Mary followed them. She watched the long, cylindrical body of her husband thrashing on the gurney. The way he wiggled and squirmed made her feel sick again. He looked like a terrible special effect in one of those really crappy, cheap horror films he loved so much.

If it had been a film, then Laurel and Hardy would have been the ideal choice to portray the slapstick antics that ensued as they attempted to get him down the stairs. Once again, it might have been funny if it hadn't been all so sad!

Eventually, they found their rhythm and managed him down the stairs. His torso kept slipping from the restraints, and the male paramedic had to stop him sliding out completely by blocking him with his hand.

Every time he slid; Mary could see the man's latex-gloved hand pushing into the flesh at the top of his head. It squished each time, and white stuff oozed between his fingers. Eventually, with much grunting and groaning, not only from Finn on the gurney but from the paramedics too, they managed to get him out of the house and into the waiting ambulance outside.

The stink followed them.

To her dismay, a gang of neighbours had gathered outside their houses, all of them vying to get a look at what was happening. She could hear the whispers, the murmurs, but did her level best to ignore them.

"Are you sure you don't want to ride in the ambulance?" the female paramedic asked, snapping her out of her revery.

"What?" she asked, feeling a little guilty for zoning out. She noticed that the paramedic, the male one, was still trying to cover his nose from the stink coming from Finn, even through his mask.

"The ambulance? Are you sure we can't tempt you to ride with us?" she asked again.

She looked down at the pathetic thing on the gurney. He was wrapped in blankets and there was a mask over what was left of his face. That was when she noticed he only had one ear, and she wondered where the other could be. She then looked at the enclosed space in the back of the ambulance. She sniffed as Finn's eye looked up at her. "Erm, no. I'll go in the car. I, erm, have to make some phone calls!"

The paramedic nodded as she pushed the gurney up the ramp, into the ambulance.

She watched them both balk at the smell.

The male paramedic stayed in the back, and the woman, removing her mask and breathing deep, closed the door and smiled at her as she made her way to the driving seat. The blue lights flashed, the siren whooped, and the large vehicle sped off down the street.

Mary glared at the neighbours revelling in the circus show before turning her back on them and going back into the house.

***

As she got into the car, she turned the ignition. She knew it was a left turn to head towards the hospital, but a right turn would take her to her mother's house, where her children were. For a moment, she thought she might go that way. The daydream was back, where she realised how easy it would be to just drive to her mother's, collect the kids, then disappear into the distance, never to be seen again.

She indicated left, then she pulled onto the road and headed towards town, following the signs for the hospital.

CHAPTER
—11—

Mick tried to move his arms, but they were just too heavy. Or were they? He could no longer tell. All he knew was he couldn't move them. He could feel them, he could bend them a little, he could even twitch his fingers, but the limbs wouldn't, or couldn't, move from the side of his body.

He tried his legs.

They were the same. It felt as if they were fused together.

He knew he'd shit himself; he also knew something bad was seeping from his penis. His insides were churning. Something was moving around in there. He'd read a story, years and years ago, about a greedy boy who'd stolen his sister's gingerbread man. After he had finished it, it reformed inside him and ran around in his belly, making him sick. He imagined this was how that felt. Like there was a little man, or an animal, or even some kind of insect, running about, turning his insides into mush.

Mush that was seeping out of his cock and arse.

Anger was boiling up inside him too. *Maybe that's what turning me into mush,* he thought, the humour lost on him as a red mist covered his eyesight. Only he didn't think it was a red mist, he thought it was his eyesight failing. The pain in his sockets was almost unbearable, and his sight had started to dim hours ago.

He could see Paula, though.

Yeah, he could see her in the corner of the room. She was cowering, crying, hugging herself as if what was happening to him was happening to her too. *It's not, though, is it?* he thought with malice. *This has to be her fault, though. I bet I caught this from her. Fucking dirty slag.*

He tried to shout at her, but he'd lost his tongue earlier. It had just slipped out of him like the thick clumps of flesh he'd vomited up. Right after his arse had collapsed.

Mick knew he was dying. He could feel his body getting thicker. He could feel the rash on his flesh pressing in on him. His body was squeezing his internal organs, forcing them out of his body.

He wondered how he was still alive.

Still, all he wanted to do was move his arms. He wanted to clench his hands into fists and plough them into his *cunt of a wife's* face.

All he could do was bark at her. *I sound like a fucking seal,* he growled in his head. *Just give me a horn and I'll make the kids laugh.*

In the middle of his barking, of him flipping and thrashing his useless body, wanting to kill the fucking bitch gawping at him, a familiar sound caused him to stop.

It was a mobile phone ringing.

Through his dimming vision, he watched as she fished out the device. She looked at the screen, and he thought her face changed. She looked relieved.

"Mary... Oh, Mary, thank fuck you've rang," she cried into the device.

Mary, he thought. *Another useless cunt! What the fuck is that dithering hag going to do to help? Her fucking husband is just as bad. He's caused all of this. If I see him, I'll fucking kill the prick!*

"Mary, It's Mick. He's really bad. I think he's—"

What? What is he doing? He snapped, barking at her. As he did, thick bile dribbled from his tongueless mouth.

"No, he's not dying, Mare! He's... he's, oh fuck, I don't know what he is. He stinks, really bad. I've called an ambulance. He's covered in—"

You lying bitch! You haven't called an ambulance. You've just been sitting there, watching me suffer. I'm going to fucking kill you, you slut, when I get out of this...

"Dial nine-nine-nine right away! Tell them It's a fucking emergency. Mare, what the hell did these two drink on Sunday night?"

Something happened inside him again. Something bad.

There was sudden agony in his chest as he felt the pressure there—which had been a constant companion since this morning—intensify. His whole body felt heavier, duller. The stress in his head was intense, and he could feel his eyes bugging from their sockets. His pleading, angry face regarded her again as she frantically pressed three numbers on her phone.

He could see her looking at him. There was fear etched into her features, there was horror in them too, but what he hated her more for, what he would quite happily get up off the floor if he could and drive a knife deep into one of those eyes for... was the pity.

CHAPTER
—12—

Mary was allowed to park her car in the Ambulance Only bays and was ushered into the back of the Emergency Unit through a different doorway than she would have entered if she were coming in as a normal emergency.

Normal emergency, she thought. *So, what kind of emergency does that make me?*

Gingerly, she opened the door and stepped inside. It was a long corridor that was very busy, filled with people doing important things, running around in nurse and paramedic uniforms, pushing full and empty gurneys here and there. She stood, alone, clutching her handbag as if it was an anchor to her past life. She felt lost and very small indeed.

"Mrs. Squires?"

The voice spooked her, and she jumped, banging into the wall behind her.

A woman with a pleasant face was smiling at her, and it instantly put her at ease, or as much at ease as she could feel under the circumstances.

"Are you Mrs. Squires?" the woman in the nurse scrubs asked, reaching out and touching her arm.

Mary nodded. A million and one questions she had been ready to ask were swallowed, lost in this one small gesture of kindness.

It was obvious she had been apprised of the situation. She gestured towards a small team who were waiting just inside the corridor. They ushered her into a small room. There was a gurney inside. Whatever it was on the trolley, whatever it had turned into, it was no longer Finn.

The oxygen mask that had been placed over what remained of his face was ill-fitting as the elastic had no ear on one side to sit correctly. The small parts of flesh that she could see looked like tinned Spam. That was all she could think of. It was unnaturally pink, and there was a white coating of grease covering it. The stink was horrendous, and with deep embarrassment and shame, she wondered how the ambulance driver and the paramedic had made it through the journey without vomiting.

She learned, via hushed tones, that they hadn't, and they were now taking their ambulance off-line for a few hours to sterilise it before further use.

The nurse who had welcomed her gestured towards the small assembled gang. Her face changed from sympathetic to business-like in the wink of an eye. It was obvious to her that this woman was in charge.

"People," she addressed them. "I think we have an SDK499 situation here. Finnley Squires, he's forty-two years of age. He has been suffering these effects for just over forty-eight hours now." She turned to Mary and the sympathetic face, the one Mary was growing to hate, was back. "That's correct, isn't it?"

Mary's eyes flicked from the woman to Finn and then back to the woman. She nodded, her voice lost again.

"Come with us," the nurse, or doctor, or whoever she was, half whispered. Mary realised that it wasn't a request, as the team was already pushing her husband away, through more doors, to God only knew where.

"What does SDK499 mean?" she asked, her voice little more than a scratch in the open wound of what was happening in the room. No one heard her question. Instead, she was ushered, rudely, through more doors and into a set of lifts. One of the nurses pressed the button for the eighth floor, and the doors closed.

Everyone in the carriage, including Mary, was uncomfortable at the smell emanating from her husband.

"Jesus Christ," one of the doctors stated as he covered his nose. He flashed Mary an embarrassed look before turning away. All she could do was smile her own embarrassed reply.

She looked around the large carriage, noting none of the team, including the woman, or nurse, who had greeted her at the entrance, were wearing any form of PPE. *Maybe It's just an allergic reaction,* she thought in an attempt to lift her spirits.

Deep down, in her own inner sanctum, she knew it was *not* an allergic reaction.

Through the short journey, the team was chatting among themselves. She could only understand maybe one word in three, as it was all medical terms, but each word she could understand worried her more and more. The words ICU, arrest, lesions, and even terminal were banded between them in hushed tones, along with the ever-worrying SDK499.

Mary was reduced to a spectator in a world she didn't, couldn't, understand. All she could do was watch with petrified eyes.

Eventually, the doors slid open, and Finn was wheeled out of the stinking lift and along a corridor towards a door that looked like it led to a secure ward. One of the team used a fob on her hip to open the door. Without further ado, they all ushered into the new corridor.

"Are you sure you want to stay?" the nurse who had fobbed in asked her. Her face was kind but serious. "It may be a little…" she paused, and Mary saw it wasn't for dramatic effect but for time to finish what she was going to say. "…overwhelming," she concluded, nodding.

Mary swallowed.

The nasty feel of grease lining the roof of her mouth made her wince. She felt disgusting, dirty, like she'd done a twelve-hour shift in the burger bar she worked in during her sixth-form years. She looked at Finn on the gurney. The small gash at the bottom of what little face he had left was open. Thick white gunk was bubbling from it, pushing the ill-fitting oxygen mask to an even jauntier angle than it had been before. Somehow, she managed a small smile.

"He's my husband," she whispered. "I'll stay!"

The nurse nodded, held her shoulder for a few strange moments, then turned back to attend to what was happening on the gurney.

Once the filth coming from Finn's mouth was wiped away and the mask was re-fitted, they all entered a room.

Inside was almost silent.

The silence was only punctured by the sounds of the team and the electronic *pings* from other closed rooms within the darkened space.

They rushed into a smaller room that was just as dim as the other. This one was adorned with more machinery than Mary had ever seen outside of an episode of *ER* on the TV. The door closed automatically behind her, and she watched as two of the men struggled to removed Finn from the gurney and place him onto the long bed in the centre of the room.

There was an ugly slurp as they lifted his strange body, and two of the team had to reach over and pull the sheets off his body as whatever he was secreting had soaked through them. Hot cheese-like tendrils clung from him to the sheets, almost as if they didn't want his body to be removed from them.

She caught a glimpse of his back; it was only for a moment, but it was enough to send her tumbling towards the edge of some insanity ridden world where wives' husbands turned into horrible, gross, disgusting *things* overnight, leaving them in a living Hell, or maybe even limbo, or wherever she was right now.

The flesh was mottled. It was discoloured and raised. It looked like he had grown an extra layer of thick, pink, brown, and, in places, purple, skin. His bloating was worse than when she had found him, and his arms were either shorter or were stuck, maybe even fused, to the rest of his body. There was very little flexibility in his movements, and it seemed to her that the two men lifting him were lifting a large, slimy log rather than the man she loved from when she was a young girl.

The noises were breaking her heart.

Each time they moved him, he wailed. He didn't shout, they were just low-key, high-pitched wails. They sounded painful, mournful, but worst of all, pitiful.

She had to turn away. The tears streaming from her eyes needed to fall. They had been threatening for a while, and seeing him like this, like a vegetable—*or maybe he's just a lump of meat*—made her both sick and ashamed for feeling that way.

The hand on her arm was meant to comfort her, but it made her feel nothing. All she could see and sense were doctors and nurses wresting a lump onto a bed. And, of course, there was the lump's pathetic protesting.

"Listen, you can still step outside if you want," a female voice whispered in her ear. "No one will think any less of you for it. We understand this must be... distressing."

Mary shook her head. "No," she replied, amazed her voice sounded so solid, so assured. "He's my husband. I need to be here for him."

However, as the nurse, or the doctor, or whatever she was, ushered her out of the door and out the other room into the corridor, she didn't resist. In fact, she was grateful for the insistence of the woman.

In the gloom, Mary cried.

***

"Oh fuck!" one of the doctors gasped as the covers were pulled away from Finn's body.

The rest of the room was silent as they observed the... well, no one knew exactly what it was anymore. It was barely human; it was barely humanoid. What was left of his face, one eye and one ear, were the only features on a desolate landscape. His nose had either flattened or the new thick dermal layer that had grown over his whole body had enveloped it. His gaping, lipless mouth was nothing more than a gash, his chin fused with the new flesh, and the white coating of grease covered the whole of his trunk-like body.

His arms were nothing but paddles stuck to the sides of his body, and his legs were fused together while the alien flesh covered them, merging him into one long, sausage-like torso. His sexual organs were lying on the bed next to the body. There was no blood where they lay, just more of the grease. The small, flaccid penis tapered to a fine point where it had been pushed out of the body, and the testicles lay independent of each other next to it. All three organs were shrivelling and turning a dark brown.

"Can we get them removed?" the doctor who had uncovered the body asked, pointing to the offending organs. It wasn't a request.

A nurse with a plastic box and extra thick gloves on picked them up and deposited them inside. She peeled a sticker from a sheet and wrote Finn's name on it before attaching it to the side of it.

The doctor shook his head.

He looked at the thing beneath him and tutted. He then removed his stethoscope. He hesitated before placing it onto Finn's mottled, fat-coated chest. When he finally did, the squelching of the cold metal touching the damp skin caused many in the room to wince. He slid the end of the device over the body, continuing his search. His face was stoic and as far away from the source of the offending smell as he could manage.

"I've got no heartbeat," he whispered to his colleagues. "He's still alive, but I can't find any rhythm at all."

He removed the instrument and held it out within a finger and thumb. The nurse who had removed Finn's penis offered him a stainless-steel container, and he dropped it inside. Everyone in the room jumped as the metal clanged against metal. He looked at all the covered faces around the room. His eyes searching for help from anyone.

"Nurse, how are we going with that saline drip?" another other doctor asked, not taking his eyes off the bizarre patient.

A middle-aged man moved forward, holding a large needle and looking unsure of himself. He smiled at the rest of them team in the room, only the smile made him look demented rather than professional. "Erm, I'm going to need to find a vein," he explained as the doctor stepped back, out of his way.

The man gulped as he stood over Finn's body. His expression told the room that he was really struggling with this job and would have given anything to be anywhere else.

The doctor just nodded pleasantly and pointed to the patient.

The nurse began to poke around what was left of Finn's arm. He grabbed the limb and attempted to lift it, to bring it closer to him to look for a nice thick vein to puncture and get the drip working. But he couldn't. The arm was stuck to the side of the man's body. He pulled a little harder, aware that everyone in the room was watching him.

The noise as the arm separated from the rest of the body was disgusting. It was wet, like the sound fresh beef makes when dropped onto a counter. He looked around at the rest of the team;

their faces, what he could see of them, were all the same, even the doctor's, who he guessed had seen a lot of disgusting shit in his years of medicine.

A new sound emerged, other than the wet tearing of the flesh and the gasping of the team; this one was someone screaming.

The nurse scrambled backwards, still gripping the patient's arm. With another sickening squelch and a horrific *snap,* a sound the poor man would remember for the rest of his life, the patient's arm came away.

The nurse found himself falling. It was only for a few disorienting moments before something solid slammed into the back of his head.

It was the floor.

As he opened his eyes, there was something on his face. It was warm, and it smelt like nothing he had ever smelt before in his life. He sat up in a flash and flung the *thing* from him. It landed two feet from where he was sitting. As he looked at the arm, the screaming sound he could hear began to make sense. It was coming from him and the patient. Thick white fat oozed from the limb, pooling around it on the floor as the flesh began to shrink, almost dry before his and the team's very eyes.

He looked up at the team. His colleagues, the people he trusted. No one was looking at him. No one was offering him any help to get up from his prone position. Their focus was on the rapidly rotting limb or the screaming patient on the bed.

"I think we're going to need to sedate the patient," the doctor said, almost absently, as his eyes flicked from Finn to Finn's arm on the floor.

Another nurse stepped forward. She was holding a larger needle than the first nurse, who was picking himself up from the floor.

"We can't have the poor man in pain," the doctor continued.

As the nurse stepped up to the bed, the patient's wide eye turned to look at her. His screams were high-pitched and pathetic, but they were genuine.

This woman's guile was obviously stronger than the male nurse's, and she showed no signs of repulsion as she attempted to prick the screaming *thing's* skin.

"It's not happening," she reported back. "I can't penetrate the skin." She was stabbing at the flesh with her needle while dancing out of the way of the white filth pouring from the wound where his arm used to be.

"Stand aside," the doctor ordered. The nurse complied.

"Do you think It's SDK499?" another of the team asked; it was the same woman who had welcomed Mary into the hospital.

"It's either that or LDK649," he replied, his gloved hands stroking his chin as he mused over the patient.

"We have an LDK649 in room twelve," the woman replied, almost mimicking the doctor's stance. "I think we need to x-ray," she continued.

The doctor was nodding absently as he watched the stump that used to be Finnley Squires screaming and thrashing on the bed.

The screaming stopped abruptly, as did the thrashing. Every set of eyes in the room were fixed upon the spectacle, or lack of, before them. The patient flopped back onto the bed, his mouth nothing more than a wide gaping gash into a toothless black hole.

The room was silent.

No one even breathed.

Eventually, a small noise broke the silence. It was barely there, only in the background, yet it was consistent, unbroken. It sounded like a motor humming, maybe a distance away but getting closer. It was a few moments before anyone in the room noticed it was getting louder, by then, no one was taking much notice of it as the trickle of thick, white drool that had been dripping from the patient's mouth was now bubbling.

It wasn't saliva, that much was obvious, it was moving much too slow to be that.

It was fat.

Cold, thick, off-white fat.

And it was stinking the room out.

"SDK499," the doctor whispered; his face had a ghost of a smile on it; it was on his lips and in his eyes. "It *is* SDK499. I've never seen one up close."

Then the noise stopped, only to be replaced by a muffled cough.

"Everyone, out of the room, now," the doctor ordered.

The team looked at him as if they hadn't understood the order.

"I said out! NOW!" He was the first to the door, and as he turned the handle and pulled it, it wouldn't open.

The coughing from the patient began to get louder, deeper, wetter.

The doctor pulled at the door with all his might, but all he could do was rattle it in its frame. "Shit," he muttered, looking back at the patient, and at the team.

He heard it before he saw it.

It *was* wet. It was the same sound a COPD patient might make after a particularly bad fit of coughing. Whatever it was that had been spat during the fit was heavy enough to make a noise as it splattered onto the hard floor.

The groans from the team told him everything he needed to know.

It was nasty.

He turned to look.

He wished he hadn't.

Never in his twenty-eight years of doctoring had he ever seen anything like this before. Lying on the floor was a thick swathe of dark blood, so dark it was almost black. Within the viscus splatter was something heavy, something meaty.

He knew exactly what it was.

It was a chunk of lung.

Another coughing fit ensued from the bed, and more chunks came flying from the patient's slash. Other things were coming from other orifices too. A string of white intestine began to snake out of the small hole within the apple of his prolapsed rectum. Something was attempting to crawl out of the vacant hole where the patient's genitalia had been.

It looked to him like the man's spleen, although he could have been wrong.

The man was trying to scream, but his mouth was full of lung. It was spongy, but it looked bunged with the same fat that was seeping out from all over this poor thing.

The nurse who had ripped the patient's arm off ducked to avoid the chunk hitting him.

He was too late. He had his mouth open at the time, screaming. The chunk of fat-clogged gristle slapped him across his face. It slipped into his waiting mouth, and involuntarily, he swallowed most of it. In his panic, he slipped on the mess on the floor and fell onto his back, swallowing the rest of the morsel.

"Grab him," the doctor shouted as he continued to rattle the door and the patient continued to cough up his innards.

Lung, liver, pancreas... his body was rejecting, giving up everything it could.

Reduced to nothing more than a slab, the patient's body convulsed and thrashed on the bed. More dripping masses flew from his mouth, others were slipping from the open, fat-oozing wound where his sexual organs used to be, and there were now all kinds of hideous monstrosities seeping from his anus, dripping off the bed and onto the floor.

The patient's screams were lost in the choking and the screams from the team who were trying their best to get out of the room, forfeiting every modicum of their professional dignity.

The doctor was screaming too, attempting to get the attention of anyone outside the room who could come and unlock the door. "Why is this fucking thing locked? *How* is it locked?" he shouted.

The nurse who had attempted to administer the painkillers strode to the door, pushing the doctor out of the way. She gripped the handle, turned it, and pushed it open.

She fell forwards as the rush of medical professionals surged from their confinement, hastening their exit, trying to put as much distance between themselves and the *thing* expelling on the bed.

It was a comical moment as six people fell out of the room, all of them helpless as they pushed to get out. The nurse's face was crushed onto the hard floor as the doctor fell upon her, as he was in turn fallen upon by the others.

Finally, a middle-aged man dressed in green scrubs flew out of the room. His face was covered in blood, and heavy vomit was exploding from his mouth, covering the helpless others.

***

Mary had been sat in the corridor for well over an hour. Even though she was nervous, scared... petrified even, hunger had caught up with her. She needed to get something into her stomach, and she needed to call her mother, to talk to the kids, to reassure them their life hadn't turned into one horrible episode of the weirdest TV programme they could think of.

As she turned the corner, heading back to her chair outside his room, complete with a nutty chocolate bar and hot, disgusting cardboard coffee, a man ran past her.

He was middle-aged and wearing green scrubs. She thought she'd seen him somewhere before but couldn't think where. There was something all over his face and down the front of his clothes.

It looked like a mixture of blood and vomit.

She dropped her hot coffee, not even registering the scalding heat as the steaming liquid poured over her thin work shirt. The chocolate bar went too as recognition dawned and she remembered where she'd seen the bloody nurse before.

"Finn..." she gasped, slipping on the coffee at her feet.

***

"Mary?"

The mad woman in the coffee-soaked shirt looked up from the floor where she was paddling in spilt warm drink. Her eyes were wide, and she couldn't focus properly.

"Not you too," Paula sobbed as she rushed to help her friend up from the floor.

Her eyes were stinging from news she had just received, and her head was throbbing. She'd needed air. The doctor who had told her it was only a matter of time before her husband, Michael, would be dead, had wanted someone to accompany her on her quest for food, but she had refused point-blank. She needed time alone, to attempt to make sense of what had been happening, and what was currently happening.

"Paula?"

Mary's voice was weak, croaky, but it was familiar. Hers had been the same when she had been given the news.

"Mary, come here." The itchy sting was back behind her eyeballs. It felt like hay-fever, like she wanted to remove the eyeball and just scratch the back of it. Tears welled, and the sight of Mary attempting to get up from the dark puddle on the floor blurred.

As Mary got up, her eyes were frantic. It was obvious she didn't care that her hair was covered in coffee and that her blouse was now totally transparent. All Paula could do was wrap her arms around her wet friend, not caring about the cooling coffee sinking into her own clothes.

"Wh-what's SDK499?" Mary asked between her own sobs. "What is it, Paula?"

At the mention of the word, Paula stopped her hug and pushed Mary away, just enough so she could see her face. "What?"

Mary wiped tears from her eyes with a shaking hand. "SDK499," she repeated, this time without the wobble in her voice. "That's what they said Finn's got. SDK499."

"LDK649," Paula said, more to herself than to her distraught friend.

Mary shook her head. "No, SDK—"

"No, I heard you," Paula soothed. "But they told me, or they mentioned while I was there, that Mick had LDK649. I've never heard of anything like that before."

Mary gulped. "The nurse. He ran past me, there was blood, and... and vomit all over him. I know something bad is—"

"Mick's not going to make it," Paula said, cutting Mary off. Once she said it aloud, it didn't feel as alien to her as it did when someone had said it to her. It felt like she was coming to peace with it.

Mary's face fell. The colour drained from it, her skin tone turning green.

"They won't let me see him. They told me to make my peace with the situation. They told me its better if I don't—" Her sob stole the rest of her words from her mouth.

It was Mary's turn to offer the hug.

Both women, both soon to be widows, hugged each other in the corridor. They hugged and cried for so long that neither of them noticed the janitor who came and wiped up the split coffee around them, placing a yellow sign next to them.

The sign read, WARNING: WET SURFACE.

"**S**ubject James, Finnley," the doctor said as he adjusted the microphone hanging over the body on the table in the centre of the room. "Body secreting a fatty substance. It is covering every inch of exposed flesh. The flesh itself is covered in a raised, discoloured rash. The rash is wet and sticky, but as it dries, it changes composition, it adds to the fatty composite. The stickiness looks to have fused the upper limbs to the torso and also fused the lower limbs together. The torso, as a whole, looks to have become one single slab."

The doctor paused for a moment. He looked up at the ceiling and took in a deep breath before continuing.

"Scans indicate a thickening of the dermal layers. This thickening has resulted in facial trauma, resulting in the loss of an eyeball, possibly due to excess pressure. It has also caused the loss of both ears. The eyeball and one of the ears were lost prior to admittance to hospital. There is a team in the home now, retrieving the items. This pressure has also caused anatomical losses. The tongue and the sexual organs have become victims to this phenomenon. It has also caused internal trauma to vital organs. It looks to have crushed the internal skeleton almost to the point that the bone structure is barely there. This, with the expulsion of the vital organs via the mouth, the anus, and *other* orifices, has caused severe respiratory problems. This is the second case within twenty-four hours. Although we believe this case to be an SDK499, the other case was more severe, and possibly more painful for the patient. We believe that one to be an LDK649. I have people monitoring for more cases, but we believe this does not offer contagion."

He clicked the recorder off and looked around at the other members of his team. "Has anyone got anything else to offer?" he asked.

Everyone in the room looked at each other. Their blank faces made the doctor smile, but only on the inside. "OK then. If no one has anything else to offer, then I think it might be time to inform the spouses of the passing of their husbands."

There was a round of nods and a general murmur of agreement.

"Nurse O'Malley," the doctor said; the smile on his face was professional, but there was something else in there too.

The middle-aged nurse, who had changed his scrubs since swallowing the expelled gristle from the patient and vomiting all over himself, looked up. There was no smile on his face.

"Have you been looked at after swallowing the... erm, expulsions?" the doctor asked.

O'Malley was visibly uncomfortable with the scrutiny of the room. He pulled the bottom of his scrubs flat and nodded. "I have, Doctor."

"And?"

The man shook his head. "Clean, sir. There was nothing wrong with me."

The doctor nodded. His professional smile spread across his face one more time. "Good. I bet you're relieved?" he asked, raising his eyebrows in a friendly manner.

"I am, Doctor. Thanks for asking."

The doctor tutted and flapped his arms at the assembled team before him. "Well then, that's that then. Only one more thing to do."

As the team were set to leave, they stopped and looked at him.

"O'Malley," the doctor said cheerily.

O'Malley's eyes rolled to the back of his head just before turning to look at the doctor again. "Yes, sir?"

"Would you be so kind as to call them?"

The nurse exhaled through his nostrils. He could feel the relief of the other members of the team, almost as if it was a physical weight lifted off them and dumped onto him. "Yes, Doctor," he replied, his voice almost a whisper.

CHAPTER
—14—

The reek was making him more than queasy.

It smelt like what he imagined a decaying body did, one that had been left in the back of a burger van on a hot roadside in one of those silly films Mary enjoyed. Was it possible for a smell to be warm? He didn't know, but his was. It was warm, sickly sweet, greasy, but most of all, it was wet.

His arms had cramped up, but he couldn't move them to wriggle or stretch it away. He tried desperately as the agony intensified, but neither limb would move. One felt like it was stuck to something, stuck so fast it was impossible to move, and the other felt like... well, it felt like it wasn't there.

He tried to move his legs, but once again, there was nothing. All feeling from below the waist was fuzzy at best. He couldn't feel much except the searing burn of cramp that was now creeping, reaching, clawing through his whole body.

The burn turned into an itch.

It was no normal itch, it was an internal itch, one he knew would never be able to be scratched, no matter how hard he tried. *If I could try,* he thought.

It was a painful itch.

He had nothing to really liken it to, but the thought occurred to him that it might be like things, important things, dissolving inside him. Things he thought he needed, you know, to survive. Fuck that, he *knew* he needed them.

What is happening to me? He wanted to shout, to yell at the top of his voice, to roar like a lion, only he couldn't because his mouth wouldn't open properly.

The panic that had been bubbling inside him, waltzing with the cramps and the itches, took its bow and decided to go solo. It won the battle with his other sensations and held dominion inside him. It made him want to thrash, to run and scream. It made him want to lash out and hit someone, anyone. It made him want to cry.

Yet he could do none of those things.

He was a prisoner, trapped in a stinking, burning, itching world there was no escape from.

Memories ran playfully through his head.

Mary, his children, the two boys. Drinking and laughing in the pub with his mates.

Threatening the old couple. Having a go at the bar staff. Insulting and laughing at the man in the kebab shop.

Inwardly, he groaned, mostly because there was no way he could groan outwardly anymore. He couldn't move his mouth, his arms, his legs. The fucking itch inside him was eating away at him, wiggling like a worm. *No, a fucking snake,* he thought. *One of those huge bastards they show you on films and internet videos.*

Open your eyes, Finn.

He didn't even know if this thought had come from him or if it was from some external source.

Open your eyes, Finn.

Breathing was a problem. His nose was buried in something that stank to high Heaven, and since he couldn't use his mouth, it was his primary source of oxygen. Each time he breathed, he was assaulted with the smell of the room, of himself. However, there was something else, something below the stink. It was another smell familiar to him.

Alcohol.

Open your eyes, Finn, the voice commanded again.

He didn't want to open them. He didn't know if he could open them. He didn't even know if he still *had* eyes to open. The voice was doing its best to soothe the panic inside him, and he could feel it subsiding, just a little. It was still bubbling just under the surface, but he thought he had a better grip of it.

You can't open your eyes, Finn... he knew this voice was his. *You can't open them because this is a dream. All of this is just a bad dream. You're feeling guilty for what you did to those nice people and the nice man in the kebab shop.*

This is all a dream.

Open your eyes, Finn.

The voice *was* his own, and he knew that, somehow, he had to obey it. Sooner or later, he needed to open his eyes, to prove to himself that this was all a figment of his imagination. His mum had always told him he had a vivid imagination, and this was proving her right.

He wished she were here right now. He wished he was a little scared boy in his bed and his mum was sat next to him, holding his hand, singing a little lullaby.

He focused all of his will to do it, found that he could.

He didn't know if it was his eyes that opened, but light shone in from somewhere. At first, it stung. It itched so bad that he began to thrash again, to move his arms—or was it arm, singular, now?—to scratch, to rub away the agony. But he couldn't. All he could do was try to work through it, let the ugly sensation pass.

Eventually, it did.

Shapes, colours, everyday sensations came flooding into his head. He was looking up at a plain beige ceiling, or a wall, he couldn't tell which. He also couldn't tell how far away from it he was as there was very little depth perception available to him. He remembered his uncle Charlie, he wasn't his real uncle, but his secret uncle. He used to come around and keep his mother company while his father was away with the army. He had lost an eye. It wasn't long after his father came back for good and he kind of stopped coming around for a bit. When he was older, he had bumped into him in the pub, and they'd had a drink together. Charlie had told him that since he lost his eye, he had problems driving as he'd lost all depth perception.

Has that happened to me?

Realisation was dawning that this was not a dream. It was very real, and very serious.

He tried to move again, but he couldn't feel anything. It was like there was no shape to him anymore, no definition.

He had become a mound.

A useless clump of flesh.

He could hear something.

It sounded like someone talking.

They were saying something about slicing into his dermal layer.

Dermal layer? Isn't that my skin? Why don't they just say skin? he thought.

They were talking about testing it, sending it somewhere to see what it was.

It's me, he wanted to shout, but, of course, he had no breath; for all intents and purposes, he had no mouth either. He wanted to grunt, to lash out, to let them know he was listening, he could hear them...

He wanted them to know he was still alive!

He was just a lump.

A lump that was alive, sentient, in pain, in agony.

He had endured the torture of his cock falling off, his tongue slipping from his mouth... *My fucking liver passing through where my dick used to be!* He guessed they thought he was dead and therefore were not going to bother administering painkillers.

Yet he needed them. He would have sold his soul for something to dull the suffering of everything that was happening to him. His bones were grinding, snapping, slowly, dissolving... perhaps even shifting. Slivers of bone, that he thought of as glass, were piercing him from the inside. Millions if not billions of little mouths, nipping, biting, eating him alive.

His blood was thickening. It was pumping slower through his strange new body. It was too thick for the veins that carried it, and he could feel them ripping, tearing as the lumps of grease oozed through him.

His arse has pushed out through his hoop. He had heard one of them sniggering when no one else was around. They were saying his arse looked like a baboon's. Bright red and swollen.

MY DICK HAS FALLEN OFF...

He wanted to die. *Or wake up!*

He was stuck. There wasn't a prolapsed muscle in his body he had control of. His brain was basically the only thing working, that and his central nervous system. He knew that due to the severe hurt he was currently enduring.

A stinging sensation cut into what used to be his stomach. At first, it was just cold, then nothing more than a scratch. But it got deeper, and pain travelled with it.

It was a knife, and it was slicing into him.

This was intense, worse than the crushing of his bones and the grating of his organs, worse than his tongue slipping out of his mouth and curling up next to him. He tried to scream, but again, nothing happened. There was no noise, no breath.

There was nothing.

How am I still alive? He sobbed, but there were no tears. There was no noise. He was now just a conscience trapped in a sensitive slab of meat.

The beeps he could hear from the room stopped, culminating into one long beep.

Everyone in the room stopped talking.

Finn knew what it meant.

It meant the machines he was hooked up to thought he was dead.

Suddenly, there were hands all over him. He could feel the anxiety in the air. Fingers prodded him; cold pads were attached to him. Strange faces loomed over him, blurred, unrecognisable. Only their concern, their interest, and their frustration registered with him.

He needed to scream. He had to reach out, to grab at them, to pull them close and whisper his hell into their ears.

Even though he was surrounded by these people, could sense them running and fussing around him, fussing, whispering, shouting orders, he couldn't have been more alone.

He had never been alone before. He was from a medium sized family, a couple of brothers, all older than him. He had many cousins and a lot of friends... But right now, there was no one. No one even knew he was still alive. No one could hear him. There wasn't one person he could reach out to.

A line from a film sprang into his head. A film he'd loved from when he was a child, and it had scared him more than anything else. It was the film in the spaceship, where the alien was running around killing everyone in sight.

He felt like that tagline now. Only he would have changed it.

When you're dead, no one can hear you scream!

He wanted to laugh at that. He thought it would have been a pretty good title for a book.

He longed for Mary, he longed for his boys. He wanted to feel them in his arms, to smell their hair as they hugged him. He missed the moistness of Mary's lips when she kissed him.

But they were not here, no one was. No one!

Every throb of his misplaced, or compressed, *or even fucking missing, to be honest,* heart sent another wave of pain through his tortured body.

They don't know I'm still alive.

The fussing continued, and more people poured into the room. The anxiety around him surged, it caused his heart, or whatever was left within him, to smash. Faster and harder it went, surging more agony through what was left of his body.

His whole universe was what he could see above him, and he felt he was even losing that. The helplessness, the loneliness, the panic, the fear, they all defined him.

He had never, ever, in all his life envisioned dying like this.

"Stop... stop! Everybody stop what you are doing!"

This voice scared him more than anything else.

"I'm calling it," the deep male voice shouted. "I'm calling it. This poor bastard has had enough. He's dead. There's nothing more we can do for him. Time of death, seven forty-eight p.m. Good job, everyone. This was a tricky one. Let's not beat ourselves up over this, we did all we could. I'll inform the wife. Nurse O'Malley, did you get in touch with the buyer?"

"I'M NOT DEAD," Finn screamed, unfortunately, only in his head.

"I'M NOT DEAD!" he screamed again. "I'M NOT DEAD... CAN'T YOU FUCKING HEAR ME?"

The world turned white as something was pulled over his face. A few moments later, there was the sound of someone laughing before the room went dark and silent.

***

He had no idea how long he had been there, silently screaming, crying. He had prayed for death. Pleaded for it. He screamed at the devil, he snivelled to God. He no longer cared who took him, just as long as someone did.

No one came.

He was forgotten. A lost soul. A tortured spirit doomed to float in the ether, to roam the in-between, alone... forever alone.

Time was meaningless. His existence was pain, agony, darkness, and the madness of despair. He could feel things seeping from him. He could no longer open his eye, or whatever it was that worked as an eye. He thought he had lost an eye, or maybe even both of them, somewhere along the way. He didn't think they had fallen out, but he had the feeling it had sunk into his face.

Suddenly, there was a blinding light.

St Peter? he thought, happy in the realisation he had finally died. Only, if he was dead, he didn't think he would still be smelling the stink still rising from him or feel the sweet torture of his innards shifting, squeezing, and snapping.

It was a few moments before he realised that the light wasn't the blessed warmth of Paradise but merely the sheet that was covering him being pulled away.

The glare from the overhead lights burned his recessed eye. It made the images before him blur. Someone was bending over him. They were looking at him, studying him. He hoped they were not here for an autopsy; he didn't think his brain could handle being cut open while conscious.

This figure was joined by another.

His heart began to pound again. He tried to move, to wriggle, to do something to show whoever it was he was still alive.

But, once again, it was in vain.

"Are they ready to go?" one of the figures leaning over him asked.

"Pretty much," the first man replied.

"Excellent," the second man said, looking back at him. There was something about this man's voice. Something he recognised.

He knows I'm still alive, Finn thought. *He really does. He knows, and I know him. I know him... I fucking know him!*

The sheet was pulled back over his face. He heard the sound of the door opening and the man, the one whose voice he recognised, whose *accent* he recognised, laugh as the door closed.

The sounds of laughter diminished, and the room fell silent again, silent except for his internal screams.

CHAPTER
—15—

He was moving.

The vibrations tore through his sensitive skin. He felt every revolution of the wheels that were pushing him; they shook him to his core, jerking him awake.

He couldn't see anything.

He could hear things, however. Footsteps and a repetitive squeaking.

Am I on a gurney? Where am I going?

He hoped it wasn't to the morgue.

He was cold, and he felt exposed. Wherever he was, he was naked. *Please don't be the morgue,* he thought again, or was it a little prayer? He couldn't tell the difference anymore. All he knew was the air around him was growing cooler, and cooler still.

He thought he might be outside.

Where am I going?

He had visions of a coffin.

He envisioned the darkness, the claustrophobic blackness of being buried alive. The never-ending obsidian of the grave. Dying slowly, in agony, short of breath, cold, the dampness of his tears mixing with the moisture of the rich soil enveloping him.

The moving sensation stopped.

He felt himself being lifted, not by hands but by something mechanical. When it stopped, the air around him was colder still. He shivered, or tried to, as he was pushed again.

The cold bit into his nakedness. It bit at his flesh, nipping him, tasting his skin before tearing it away and infiltrating his insides.

The cold become more and more intense.

Then he stopped.

There was a shuffle, and whoever it was who'd been pushing him lifted him. There was no gentleness to the movement. It was more like a rough shove and a drop. He then heard the footsteps of whoever it had been, they were walking away.

The squeaking of the wheel went with it.

A shudder ran through him.

He knew that shudder, it was the starting of a diesel engine. He was in a vehicle.

Inertia made him lurch as the vehicle pulled away, on its way to whatever was to be his final destination.

The cover over his eye fell.

What he saw before him made him scream silently.

He screamed, and screamed, and then he screamed again!

The large slab of kebab meat before him, the one that was covered in a hospital sheet, leaning against the wall of the van, had a tag hanging from it.

Finn could just about make out what it read.

Tyrell, Michael, LDK649

CHAPTER
—16—

Ozzie hauled his two new kebab slabs out of the back of his van. He dropped them onto his trolly and wheeled them into the back room of his shop. *I'm going to have to get some oil onto that,* he thought, looking at the offending wheel.

He struggled to get the trolly into the back room, where his father was cutting onions. He turned and grinned, nodding.

The old man didn't speak English, but then Ozzie had never been very good at it either.

"Is this the new *special stuff?*" the old man asked him in his ancient Latin.

"It is, Papa," Ozzie replied as he picked up the first slab and placed it on the counter. He ripped the tag off it, the one that read, Tyrell, Michael, LDK649

"Large donna kebab," Ozzie laughed, holding the sign out to his father. "Six pounds and forty-nine pence. Do you hear me?"

The old man laughed again. "Six pounds and forty-nine pence," he replied, his accent sounding odd speaking English words.

"This one was going to be a small donna kebab, four pounds and ninety-nine pence, but I'm thinking you should make it special, Papa. I think we're going to need it." Ozzie laughed again, and he hauled the hunk of kebab meat off his trolley, dumping it on the counter next to the other one. He ripped the tag reading SDK499 from it and dropped it on the floor.

He stepped back, regarding the two large slabs on his counter. He grinned. "So, tell me, boys," he whispered in his deep Greek accent. "Who's the camel jockey now, eh? Metagh!"

The last word was spat, then he pulled a deep hock from the back of his throat. He spat it into his hands and rubbed it onto the slab that used to be Mick. He then ran his greasy fingers through his hair before putting his cap back on and walking out to the front of the shop.

CHAPTER
—17—

Finn lay on the counter in the back of the shop. He couldn't move, he couldn't talk, all he could do was watch as his old friend Mick had a long metal rod inserted through him, top to bottom.

He was convinced he heard him scream.

The thought was ridiculous, but still it lingered.

Ozzie was grinning as he fixed the rod impaling his best friend to an upright gas heater.

Finn watched as the gas grills were lit and Mick began to spin.

The last thing he saw before Ozzie carried him off to the back of the shop, to where he kept the long, sharp knives, was Mick's eye, deep within the slab. It was wide, it was filled with pain, and it was scared.

A small tear in the meat appeared to drip down the slab as the top layer cooked.

Finn could see a mouth, and that mouth was screaming.

***

Ozzie laughed as the sharp knife sliced into Finn's skin.

There was a small tub on the counter next to him. There was a label on the side of it. "The Special Stuff," it read.

Ozzie's "Metagh" tub began to fill once more.

AUTHOR'S NOTES

"Large donna, extra onions, loads of tomatoes. The hottest chilli you do, yeah, loads of tahini. What? Pickle? Of course, I want a pickle…"–under my breath, *stupid question!*

I love a donna kebab. Some people will lie and say, "Nope, I could never eat one of them sober." Whenever I hear that, I see them for who they truly are, rats and snakes (just jokes BTW). I think even vegetarians and vegans could eat donna kebabs, as I honestly question the quantity, and quality, of meat in them. Long shards of curly brown goodness. It's supposed to be lamb, I think, but it has its very own *unique* taste.

Taxis hate them, your best white shirts love them, your arse reheats them the next day… they are just boss. They are the *only* reason why I could never be vegetarian.

This book is an homage to the morning after the night before. We've all had that night in the pub, drinking lager (or some other rubbish) until you can't talk anymore, and all as just the first course to the delectable banquet that is the donna kebab on the way home.

The worst hangover I have ever had lasted for three days. I had been out with the lads (I still lived at home with the fam), and I fell into the house. I woke up on my bedroom floor, and I swear I couldn't move. I mean, I could, but my brain would follow my head about 0.3333333333 seconds after, turning my stomach, making me hurl. I vomited, vomited, and then vomited some more. For three days, I couldn't eat, all I could do was sip warm water or flat coke.

None of that stopped me from going back and doing it all again the next weekend, though.

Thinking about my teenage/early twenties (now I'm nearly fifty) seriously knocks me ill. I wonder how I survived it. No wonder I never took up writing until I was well into my thirties.

Well, I hope you enjoyed reading this as much as I enjoyed writing it. I haven't tried to up the grossness levels for this one as after Zola and Cravings, I'm not sure I could… although, the little cameo in here by The Stinky Stump has gotten the old grey matter whirring!!!!

Watch this space!

***

Thank Yous and Acknowledgements

A huge thank you to Lisa Lee Tone, my editor. I always think I'm going to shock her with the stuff she edits for me, but I've not managed to, yet. Although she was a little put off with my Seagull book.

Kelly Rickard, one of the finest proof-readers I know. She reads anything I throw at her, and I've thrown some pretty spicy stuff her way.

The girls from Mothers of Mayhem–Marian, Christina, Donna, Rachel, Danika. I love your podcast. Honestly, every time my name is mentioned, I fanboy a little. I blush and grin, and everyone asks what's the matter with me! Also, Corrina, Crystal, Ryder–you guys are so supportive of my work, I honestly can't thank you enough.

Drew is a wizard. Without him and Godless, the indie horror scene would be a lost child in an amusement arcade, whose parents are in the bingo. A wandering stranger in a strange land. Keep that shit up!

To all the guys from the indie scene–too many to mention. Anna, get that Hearse of Horror up and running chicken, because It's a boss idea. Simon, Sean, Lindsey, Peter... Jesus (no, not HIM), there are just too many people to mention who have welcomed me into this extreme horror / splatterpunk family! Long may it last.

Oh, got to mention the family too. Lauren wouldn't proofread this (pussy), Grace and Sian (they've NEVER read anything I've written), Ann (my mum, she isn't allowed to read anything I write), Annmarie (she reads everything I write), and Helen (tells everyone she's read everything but really hasn't), and all the other assorted, mad, crazy, beautiful people who grace my life with their presence.

But most of all, to YOU, the reader. If you didn't read, I would probably be in prison now, not for anything cool but something stupid like causing an accident by dropping my kebab on the floor.

Anyways... keep on rocking n' rolling, and don't go changing!

Dave McCluskey
Liverpool
August 2022

ABOUT THE AUTHOR

Born in Liverpool in the UK, **Dave McCluskey** left school and began working in a music shop selling guitars and drums and playing in local bands around the Liverpool music scene. When he realized that fame and fortune, and rock god status was proving rather elusive, he went to university where he wasted almost 30 years of his life messing around with computers.

He became a novelist later on in life having been an avid reader since he was a child. He writes as DE McCluskey, mostly in the genre of horror (mainstream, extreme, and comedy), although he has been known to dabble in thrillers, romance, science fiction, fantasy, and also children's books (written as Dave McCluskey).

He began his writing career creating comics and graphic novels, thinking they would be easier to write and sell than traditional novels (how wrong he was). He then made the switch into the media of novels and audiobooks and has not looked back since.

His books include the highly regarded *The Twelve, Cravings, Zola*, and the historical thriller In *The Mood for Murder*.

Dave remains an avid football fan although sometimes he wonders why, and he has been known to lurk around the stand-up comedy circuit in the North-West of England.

He lives at home with his partner, their two children, and a sausage dog with his own future children's book series, called Ted (Lord Teddington of Netherton).

Want more stories?

You can view the entire Evil Cookie book catalog at **www.theevilcookie.com**

————————

Keep up to date on new book releases, announcements and cover reveals by following The Evil Cookie!

Facebook: theevilcookiepublishing

Instagram: theevilcookiepublishing

X: @EvilCookiePub

Blue Sky: theevilcookiepub

YouTube: The Evil Cookie Publishing

Printed in Great Britain
by Amazon